MARKING IN OR ON LIBRARY BOOKS IS
A MISDEMEANOR. (N.C. STATUTE 14-398)
IF YOU NEED TO IDENTIFY BOOKS THAT
YOU HAVE READ. PLEASE USE THIS SHEET.

Cunning Workmen

Also by Isabella Alden in Large Print:

Ester Ried Yet Speaking

This Large Print Book carries the Seal of Approval of N.A.V.H.

Cunning Workmen

Isabella Alden

Thorndike Press • Waterville, Maine

Published in 2001 by arrangement with Munce Publishing.

Thorndike Press Large Print Christian Fiction Series.

The tree indicium is a trademark of Thorndike Press.

The text of this Large Print edition is unabridged.
Other aspects of the book may vary from the original edition.

Set in 16 pt. Plantin by Minnie B. Raven.

Printed in the United States on permanent paper.

Library of Congress Cataloging-in-Publication Data

Alden, Isabella Macdonald, 1841–1930.
　　Cunning workmen / Isabella Alden.
　　　p. cm.
　　ISBN 0-7862-3382-6 (lg. print : hc : alk. paper)
　　1. Sunday-school teachers — Fiction.　2. Large type books.
　　I. Title.
　　PS1019.A5 C8 2001
　　813′.4—dc21　　　　　　　　　　　　　　　　2001027522

CONTENTS

WELCOME

by Grace Livingston Hill

As long ago as I can remember, there was always a radiant being who was next to my mother and father in my heart and who seemed to me to be a combination of fairy godmother, heroine, and saint. I thought her the most beautiful, wise, and wonderful person in my world, outside of my home. I treasured her smiles, copied her ways, and listened breathlessly to all she had to say, sitting at her feet worshipfully whenever she was near; ready to run any errand for her, no matter how far.

I measured other people by her principles and opinions, and always felt that her word was final. I am afraid I even corrected my beloved parents sometimes when they failed to state some principle or opinion as she had done.

When she came on a visit, the house seemed glorified because of her presence; while she remained, life was one long holiday; when she went away, it seemed as if a blight had fallen.

She was young, gracious, and very good to be with.

This radiant creature was known to me by the name of Auntie Belle, though my mother and my grandmother called her Isabella! Just like that! Even sharply sometimes when they disagreed with her: *"Isabella!"* I wondered that they dared.

Later, I found that others had still other names for her. To the congregation of which her husband was pastor she was known as Mrs. Alden. And there was another world in which she moved and had her being when she went away from us from time to time; or when at certain hours in the day she shut herself within a room that was sacredly known as a Study, and wrote for a long time, while we all tried to keep still; and in this other world of hers she was known as Pansy. It was a world that loved and honored her, a world that gave her homage and wrote her letters by the hundreds each week.

As I grew older and learned to read, I devoured her stories chapter by chapter, even sometimes page by page as they came hot from the typewriter; occasionally stealing in for an instant when she left the study to snatch the latest page and see what had happened next; or to accost her as her morning's work was done with: "Oh, have you finished another chapter?"

Often the whole family would crowd around when the word went around that the last chapter of something was finished and going to be read aloud. And now we listened, breathless, as she read and made her characters live before us.

The letters that poured in at every mail were overwhelming. Asking for her autograph and her photograph; begging for pieces of her best dress to sew into patchwork; begging for advice on how to become a great author; begging for advice on every possible subject. And she answered them all!

Sometimes I look back upon her long and busy life, and marvel at what she has accomplished. She was a marvelous housekeeper, knowing every dainty detail of her home to perfection. And a marvelous pastor's wife! The real old-fashioned kind, who made calls with her husband, knew every member intimately, cared for the sick, gathered the young people into her home, and loved them all as if they had been her brothers and sisters. She was beloved, almost adored, by all the members. And she was a tender, vigilant, wonderful mother, such a mother as few are privileged to have, giving without stint of her time, her strength, her love, and her companionship. She was a speaker and teacher, too.

All these things she did, and *yet wrote books!* Stories out of real life that struck home and showed us to ourselves as God saw us; and sent us to our knees to talk with him.

And so, in her name I greet you all, and commend this story to you.

Grace Livingston Hill

(This is a condensed version of the foreword Mrs. Hill wrote for her aunt's final book, *An Interrupted Night.*)

1

THE CORNER CLASS

Mr. Robert Hammond stood before his glass brushing his hair — very fine hair it was, and it crowned a handsome head. Having arranged it to his liking, Mr. Hammond proceeded to brush his clothes; little specks of dust were flying hither and thither, intent on their usual mischievous errands, and the most that Mr. Hammond did was to set a few more of them in commotion; but as that seemed the proper thing to do to complete his toilet, he conscientiously did it.

A very firm, emphatic knock sounded at his door, and, in answer to his permission to enter, a small being, done up in white furs, with a blue feather on her head — around her hat, of course — daintily stepped in and spoke rapidly and to the point.

"Uncle Rob, the bell has said, 'Come quick — come quick — come quick,' until I'm sick of hearing it, and Miss Ellsworth, Miss Warren, and lots of others have gone by, and I'm quite most certain sure that we'll be late."

"Just so," said Uncle Rob; and he proceeded in a very leisurely manner to the putting on of his rubbers.

Miss Marion drummed with her small gloved fingers on his toilet table during the operation and repeated her assurances of tardiness, and finally, with infinite satisfaction, saw him draw on his gloves and take up his books. Once in the street, the keen air did for Marion what her foreboding of lateness failed to do. Her uncle quickened his steps until her small feet were obliged to break into a decided run to keep pace with him, and a very brief space of time it took to get down Queen Street and come out on Harvard Street, where the great stone church stood, on which the deep-throated bell was loudly repeating its call for workers.

"You see, little lady, that the bell is still calling," Mr. Hammond said as they mounted the steps.

"Course," said Marion; "that's what I told you. It called and called, and we didn't come; but we're here now — I don't see why it doesn't stop."

Her uncle laughed.

"It is just possible that it thinks someone else is coming and would like to know the time," he said pleasantly.

"Then I should think they might have

found it out," said Marion positively. "Why, Uncle Rob, it has struck ten hundred times while you were getting ready, I do believe! I must have had to put my hands to my ears, it tried me so."

To this Uncle Robert made no reply. He had held a great many conversations in his life with Miss Marion, and having discovered that she was certain to have the last word anyway, it was just as well to stop then as at any future time — besides, they were at the schoolroom door. Marion dodged through an open door at one side over which hung, "Come in, Little Lambs," in dainty lettering; and straightway there was a great buzzing of little tongues and a nodding of blue, white, and scarlet plumes, as the twenty or so "little lambs" welcomed the newcomer. Mr. Hammond went around back of the rows and rows of seats arranged in semicircles until he reached the class in the west corner behind a post and under a window that commanded a view of the passersby. The people in that semicircle were in various stages of unrest. It was a bewildering sort of class. If the superintendent studied to discover how many phases of character and grades of society he could group in a number seven, he had made a decided success. Each and every one of them deserves an introduction.

In the corner sat Larry Bates; boys like Larry always *do* get in the corner, exactly behind the aforesaid post. Larry had bright eyes, curly hair, and a brain keen enough for anything earthly except to commit to memory a Sabbath-school lesson that he had never yet accomplished. Larry's home was a study in its way, if one had time for it. "How not to do it" was the art that was carried nearly to perfection in that household. To be free and easy, to go where one liked, to do what one wanted to do at all times without regard to other people's desires or necessities — this was what the family strove for, or would have striven for if it hadn't needed energy, which it had not. Always excepting Larry; no one ever accused him of lacking energy, unless indeed there was something useful to be done. Why Larry came to Sunday school was sometimes a puzzling question, even to himself. The other fellows who lived near him happened to go, and the singing was prime in that school, better than anywhere else in town, everybody knew; and — oh, well, he just happened to think he would go, and that was all Larry knew about it. I have always thought that Larry's mother, who was in heaven, knew a great deal more about it than that.

Next to him was Job Jenkins. Well named was he. If ever a boy, since the days when Job of old was a boy, had need of patience, this was he. A lovely home had Job; one of those delightful abodes that a foreigner might think we gloried in, so much do we honor the principal agent in manufacturing them — a house wherein brown paper, or old hats, or rags, took the place of window glass; where the one stove smoked all the time, when there was anything to make a smoke with; where hunger, cold, and discomfort of every name held carnival. Easy to tell why Job Jenkins came to Sunday school in the winter; at least he needed no greater inducement than the fact that it was held in a warm room, and that the warming apparatus didn't smoke.

Then there was Lester St. John. You know all about the St. Johns, of course; they live on Lester Avenue, which was named for Mrs. St. John's father, old Adam Lester, at a time when he owned the whole of it. The St. Johns have absolutely no wish unsupplied that money has anything to do with. The supply seems unlimited, is freely lavished on the children, and is ever on the increase. When you add to this statement the fact that there is not a Christian in that family, it would perhaps be difficult to find one who needed the help of Sunday-school education any more than did Lester St. John. Not that he thinks he needs anything; he is seventeen, a clear-eyed, sharp-brained, handsome lad with a very frank, genial look about him, and yet with flash enough in his bright eyes to show plainly that his own way is decidedly the way that he prefers to all others. He came to Sunday school because he was studying evidences of Christianity, and so far as intellect was concerned, was decidedly interested in the subject. A dangerous mind to handle had Lester St. John.

Will Gordon was demure and meek looking enough, but every scholar in Sunday school knew perfectly well that Will Gordon could do more good-natured mischief in less time than any other known boy, not even excepting Larry Bates himself. The difference was, he was less outspoken about it. Perhaps there was another difference; the home training of the two had been very unlike. Larry knew nothing about the Bible, and cared less. Will, intellectually, was sufficiently posted to be the minister himself, instead of his son, and cared for it all about as much as Larry did.

At the end of the seat was Peter Armstrong. He lived, or boarded, at Mr.

Randolph's. Neither father nor mother had Peter. He had what he earned every week, which was his board and good serviceable clothing. Peter was slow, steady, and patient and always had his lesson carefully prepared; so, for that matter, had Will Gordon — the minister looked after that.

There were two brothers in the class, Lewis and Arthur Sanford by name, who were newcomers, about whom very little was known, save that they were boarders and students at the academy, that they had very little pocket money, that they were good scholars, capital ball players, and kind of queer fellows somehow — all this the boys said. I think they came to Sunday school because it was one of the excellent rules of that excellent academy, that come they must. As for Peter Armstrong, he came because he wanted to.

Into this class came Mr. Hammond on the morning of which I am telling you and took his seat. The class had been his but a very short time, and as yet he hardly knew his material; if he had, I think he might have trembled. I have been thus particular in introducing these young men to you because I have several things to tell you about them; and because, also, you are likely to meet them almost any day and may as well be forearmed. Mr. Hammond shook hands cordially with each one, having a separate word for each. "Well, Larry, how is Uncle Mills this morning? Is the cough better, Jenkins? Lester, I saw your brother in the city yesterday, and he sent love." And then the bell rang, and the opening exercises were in order.

"It's a rather queer story, anyhow, the whole of it. Don't you think so, Mr. Hammond?"

This was one of the first remarks that Lester St. John volunteered concerning the lesson. Mr. Hammond smiled quietly and answered that he thought it very queer indeed. Which rather astonished and, for the time being, silenced Lester. He had not expected Mr. Hammond to say any such thing.

That gentleman appealed to Larry.

"What do you think about it, Lawrence?"

"Me!" said Larry, in good-natured amazement. Nobody ever asked him what he thought.

"Larry thinks the lesson is in the Psalms," said Will Gordon; whereupon the entire class, Peter Armstrong excepted, seemed to think it proper to laugh.

"It is," Mr. Hammond said.

"That's news to me," Arthur Sanford said. "I thought the lesson was in Exodus."

"Addition is the first rule given in arithmetic, but you find addition elsewhere through the book. There is a great deal in the Psalms about these people. St. John, we must come back to you, I think. Tell us wherein the story strikes you as queer."

"Oh, such an army of people who knew all about the Promised Land, what a splendid place it was, and they knew that the Egyptians had no business to make slaves of them! Why, they even knew they were the Lord's chosen people, and yet they stupidly worked away from day to day — worked and grumbled! Why didn't they just start up and fight for their freedom?"

"You would have done so, you think, if you had been one of them?"

"Well, I would in a hurry. There doesn't seem to be any sense in their proceedings from first to last. I've been looking ahead, you see; and of all the stupid, senseless-acting people that ever I heard of, it strikes me, they went a little ahead."

"I think them a remarkably foolish people myself; but, as for being more so than any I have ever heard of, I am not quite prepared for that. However, we will discover what we can about them."

You will have discovered before this that Mr. Hammond's class was busy with that strange old story that reads from first to last like a romance — the trials, sins, and wanderings of the children of Israel. The class was decidedly interested and expressed their opinions freely, their teacher appearing in no wise shocked by their original manner of making known their thoughts. At least, if Mr. Hammond was shocked, he kept the matter entirely to himself. The half hour was nearly over when he turned suddenly to Lester St. John with a question.

"By the way, St. John, what has become of Henry Fields?"

"He is in the office, sir; but his cough is bad, and he grows thin very rapidly."

"Still smoking?"

"Yes, sir. Father talked with him about it; asked him if he knew that the physicians thought it was killing him. But he says there is no use in talking, he can't give up cigars."

"What about *that* bondage, St. John?"

Now, every single boy in Mr. Hammond's class, except Peter Armstrong, smoked cigars. Every boy laughed; but St. John was ready with a response.

"I know what you are thinking, Mr. Hammond; but very few people are affected as Henry Fields is by a cigar. If *I* were, I should stop smoking today."

"You could do it, just as well as not?"

"No, sir; not just as well as not. I like cigars, and I should rather hate to stop smoking; but I *could* do it, and I would, if there was any occasion."

"Do you think Henry Fields could?"

"No, sir; or rather I think he thinks he can't. I see what you are coming at, and I think Fields is just as foolish as the Israelites were. I mean to have a talk with him tomorrow about these old dolts."

Mr. Hammond turned to Lewis Sanford.

"Lewis, I think you are an intimate acquaintance of young Fields. Can you give us an idea how he came under bondage to cigars?"

"Yes, sir, I think I can"; and there was a gleam of mischief in Lewis's eyes. "He told me all about it. The first cigar he ever smoked was one day when he made up his mind that he was just as good a fellow, and could stand just as much, as Lester St. John, any day."

Mr. Hammond looked at St. John.

"The Egyptians placed the Israelites in bondage," he said pointedly; "and I think you said they had no business to do so."

"And also that the Israelites had no business to stand it," said St. John quickly.

His teacher laughed.

"Yes, that is so," he said. Then he

21

glanced at his watch. "Young gentlemen, there is one question further that I want to ask each of you. You have heard St. John's opinion of the Israelites, and we seemed to agree with it. Do you know of any class of people, or of any individuals, who have been promised an inheritance, who know just what sort of place it is, yet who have sold themselves as slaves to a cruel task-master whom they hate, and, in the face of the fact that God himself has redeemed them and stands ready to lead them out, stupidly work away at their tasks?"

At that moment the superintendent's bell rang, and Mr. Hammond whirled his chair around and faced the desk.

"Of all the stupid, senseless people that ever I heard of —" began Will Gordon, quoting from his friend's unflattering opinion of the Israelites, as the two left the chapel together.

St. John laughed.

"Ah, that was only the art of putting things," he said gaily. "Mr. Hammond has that art in perfection."

Yet exactly what these two young men thought of themselves in the light of the last question put to them, they kept to themselves, as young men are quite apt to do.

2

THE BABY LESSON

The next class to Mr. Hammond's was Miss Cora Parkhurst's. That lady deserves a few words of description or comment. She was noticeable in the school by reason of her coming late. The very children along the streets had fallen into the habit of saying, "Why, there goes Miss Parkhurst; we'll be *awful* late!"

On this particular morning she was later than usual. The opening exercises were concluded, and the classes were busy with their lessons, when she rustled in. Rustled is exactly the word to apply to her. The passage between the seats was narrow, and her dark blue silk was new and heavy. Two young ladies were awaiting her arrival, Miss Celia Evans and Miss Sarah Blake. Miss Evans was the daughter of Chester Evans, the president of the Second National Bank, the first director in the iron mines, the heaviest stockholder in Evans's Mills west of town, and the important personage to be consulted in every important event, monetary, literary, or religious, that was to transpire in the town. Miss Blake was the daughter of Joseph Blake, foreman in Mr. Evans's shoe factory.

"I am late this morning," Miss Parkhurst said, whereupon Miss Evans laughed.

"Now, you are laughing because you think I always *am* late; I know you are, but you must admit that I am not often so far behind as this." Miss Parkhurst said this with that rich, good-humored smile which was hers by nature and added immediately, "Let me see; where is the lesson today?"

"I don't know, I'm sure," Miss Cora answered promptly. "I forgot my Bible, and I never *can* keep track of those lesson papers. Did you notice where they said it was, Sarah?"

Sarah was not quite sure but had some dim notion that it might be in Exodus, or possibly Deuteronomy — somewhere in that vicinity anyway.

"Dear me!" Miss Parkhurst said, in some dismay. "We ought to know where the lesson is, certainly. I haven't had time to study mine this week. Haven't you a lesson paper, Sarah?"

No, Sarah was not present on the preceding Sabbath, when the lesson papers had been given out.

"Where are the rest of the girls, I wonder?"

"Fanny and May were at the party last night. They never get out anywhere the day after a party." This information Miss Celia gave and added: "That party was a brilliant affair, Miss Parkhurst. The finest we have had this season."

"Was it?" Miss Parkhurst said with animation. "I thought it would be something special. We always do have such nice times at Mrs. Brown's. I was quite disappointed in not being able to go. Sarah, do you know where Hatty is?"

"They had extra work at the factory last night and worked until midnight finishing off a job that was promised. Hatty went home tired out, and I guess she hasn't got rested yet."

"I think that is breaking the Sabbath," Miss Parkhurst said decisively, "to run the factories until midnight on Saturday. I wonder at Mr. Peck for allowing it."

"I don't see why it is any worse than parties." This from outspoken Sarah. Miss Parkhurst laughed her sweet good-natured laugh, then she said:

"But you know, Sarah, people need not go to parties unless they choose, but keeping the factory open is sort of compelling people to get tired out."

"There is something in that," Sarah said reflectively. "Only people seem to *choose* to do it whenever they get a chance; and what's the difference anyway between the people who break the Sabbath for fun and those who break it for money, so that it gets broken by both of them?"

Miss Parkhurst did not like to be metaphysical. She smiled on the questioner, then answered kindly, "A great deal of difference, I fancy"; then added briskly, "but we really must secure a lesson paper and find out what they are all so interested in." Then she rustled her beautiful robes in between the separating aisles and accosted Mr. Hammond:

"I beg your pardon, sir, for the interruption; but have you a spare lesson paper? I find there is not one in my class."

Without note or comment, Mr. Hammond took from his pocket an extra lesson leaf, bowed silently in response to her hearty thanks, and tried faithfully for the next five minutes to renew the interest that her coming had broken.

"Now," Miss Parkhurst said, reseating herself and arranging her ruffles, "we are ready for the lesson. Let me see; what day of the month is it? Oh, it's the first Sabbath in the month, is it not? No, it is the second. Well, then, this must be the lesson about Moses. We'll read the verses first." Miss Parkhurst read her verse as her turn came, in smooth-flowing tones; then between times adjusted her bracelets and arranged her overskirt. The lesson was finally read, and the teacher betook herself to the lesson paper. Faithfully she went down the list of questions prepared by the committee to aid in the *study* of the lesson. "To what house or tribe did Moses belong?"

"I'm sure I don't know," Miss Celia said listlessly. "Does it tell in the verses?"

"I think it does. Oh, yes, you'll find it in the first verse."

Being thus directed, Miss Celia succeeded in answering the question, and Miss Parkhurst proceeded. "What was the name of the father?"

Not the slightest idea had Sarah Blake. She had never heard, or thought, or cared anything about Moses' father. She was utterly indifferent as to what his name might be. Miss Parkhurst was a trifle embarrassed.

"I really don't remember what his name was myself. Do you, Celia?"

"Mercy! No, I never knew."

"What's the use of knowing, anyway; who cares what his name was?"

Miss Parkhurst laughed. "What a practical young lady you are, Sarah; you want a reason why for everything."

"Well, but what *is* the use?"

"Why, it is pleasant to know things, isn't it? Somebody might ask you about it, and you would like to be able to tell them," which method of reasoning brought the teacher back to the present embarrassment, that she was not able to give her class the desired information; but her eyes brightened as they rested on a sentence in her paper.

"Why, there's a reference," she said, briskly. "Numbers 26:59. Have you a Bible, Celia?"

"No, ma'am; I always depend on a lesson paper."

"And I forgot mine this morning; how unfortunate! Well, never mind, we can each look that question up at home."

"I don't suppose I ever shall," said practical Sarah, "because I really don't care a straw what his name is."

Celia did not *say,* but who believes she will ever look up the name of Moses' father? Her teacher certainly gave her no motive for doing so. There were several other questions with reference answers to be passed, then the verses of the lesson furnished a few answers. Then came another puzzle: "What is the meaning of the word *Hebrew*, and how is it used?"

"I didn't know it had a meaning, any more than *and* or *it*."

"Yes," Miss Parkhurst said, with great appearance of wisdom, "all those old names had special meanings, but I don't at this moment recall the meaning of *Hebrew*. I really ought to have studied my lesson, but I had not a moment of time."

Sarah had been reading her lesson paper to some purpose. She came to their enlightenment.

"Why it don't mean anything, only what it says. It's in the sixth verse; 'This is one of the Hebrews' children.' "

"But why were they called Hebrews?" questioned Celia.

"Why am I called Sarah? You might as well ask that question."

Miss Parkhurst shook her head. "There is some special reason why they were called Hebrews, I think, though, as I said, I don't remember what it is. We will have to pass that — I'll look it up during the week."

Easy questions followed, answered by

merely reading over the verse of Scripture. Still, this process consumed some time, owing to the fact that neither teacher nor scholars knew in just which verse to look for the desired answer. Miss Parkhurst yawned behind her glove several times during the pauses, while the girls hunted. Once the yawn was so audible that it called forth an apology. "I was up late last night, and I am wretchedly sleepy this morning. I almost gave up the idea of coming to Sunday school on that account."

To do Miss Parkhurst justice, she rarely sat up late on Saturday evenings, but this had been a special occasion. Some queer idea of economy — or what she chose to consider economy — caused her to do much of her own ruffling and puffing, and the ruffles on her blue silk overskirt were not finished on Saturday evening. Now, any reasonable mortal will at once perceive that the lady could not go to church without an overskirt, and as she was equally certain that no dress but the blue silk would be just the thing to wear, she patiently sewed, setting the last stitch only five minutes before the clock struck twelve. Then there were the bastings to dispose of, and the entire suit, skirt, overskirt and basque to slip on and see if everything about them was as it should be. Then there was her hair to do up in pins. Very tired was Miss Parkhurst. She would willingly have foregone the pleasure of pulling and twisting her hair. She was very sorry that "they" wore it crimped; but since they did, what refuge was there for her but in hair pins? No lady will wonder that the clock struck one before Miss Parkhurst laid her tired, crimped head on her pillow.

As she turned out the gas, she thought of her Sabbath-school lesson, tried to recall where it had been the previous Sabbath, where it would be likely to be next, tried to remember where she had last seen her lesson paper, or if indeed she had remembered to bring one home with her, finally dismissed the whole subject with a weary yawn and a promise to herself to get up early in the morning and study her lesson, after which she went to sleep and slept hard and fast until her sister Nettie summoned her to breakfast, and the ringing bell announced that it was eight o'clock. You certainly see how she came to be late to school that Sabbath morning.

"What did the princess call the child?" said Miss Parkhurst, coming out from behind her glove to ask this question; and Sarah answered sharply:

31

"Why, Moses, of course. Miss Parkhurst, don't you think it is a very silly little lesson for great girls like us? Why, I've known all about Moses ever since I was born; and just think of those boys in Mr. Hammond's class studying this little baby lesson. I think it is absurd."

"I don't believe in uniform lessons *myself*," said Miss Parkhurst, with so much decision that the committee who worked so faithfully and laboriously to prepare them would doubtless have stopped in dismay could they have heard her. "I have always believed that different intellects demand different lessons in the Sabbath school as well as anywhere else; but uniform lessons is a pet theory of Mr. Gordon's, you know, and we must fall in with the rest, I suppose. Well, Celia, what is the meaning of the word?"

"What word, Miss Parkhurst?"

Miss Parkhurst looked more closely at the lesson paper and read the question again. "It must refer to some word in the verse just mentioned. Let me see; 'What did the princess call his name?' Oh, I see, it means Moses. What is the meaning of the word *Moses?*"

"I'm sure I don't know," Celia said, laughing. "Has my name a special meaning, Miss Parkhurst? I never thought of attaching much importance to the meaning of names before."

"Those old heathen nations used to do so, I believe."

"But Moses wasn't a heathen," Sarah Blake said sharply.

"No, certainly not; but very possibly they had fallen into the same habit."

"I think it's a horrid name," Celia said. "It's my uncle's name, too. Grandpa would insist on having him called so, his *first* name, but he never uses it, of course. He only uses the initial. M. Willard Evans he always writes his name, and it looks very well so. Do you know Uncle Willard, Miss Parkhurst?"

"I used to know him years ago, when we were both children," Miss Parkhurst answered with animation. "But I presume I should not recognize him now. I have heard he is coming very soon; is it so?"

"He has sailed, and we are hoping he will be here in time for the festival. Miss Parkhurst, do you think blue silk will be too much dressed for the festival? I am to sing, you know."

"Why, not at all. Of course those who take part will be expected to dress a good deal."

"That's what Mother told Mrs. Gordon. She harps about dress a good deal. Ministers' wives always do, you know; but I shall wear my blue silk. I think it is more becoming to me than any other color, don't you?"

"It is very becoming; but your complexion is so fair that you can wear almost any color. I think the festival is going to be a success. I hope your Uncle Willard *will* get here in time. We want to show him that we have pretty things here, as well as in Europe."

What Moses thought all this time, if it were permitted him to listen to this strange Sabbath teaching, I cannot tell you, though certainly I have thought that I will ask him, among other things, if he really did hear any of the million things that were said about him in Christendom that Sabbath day and, hearing, what he thought of Miss Parkhurst and her class. But the meek old man will have added greatly to his crowning virtue during these thousands of years in heaven. So it may be he will judge them all very gently.

Mr. Newton's bell rang before the matters pertaining to Moses Willard Evans and the festival were all arranged, and Miss Parkhurst came back with a start to the remembrance that Moses, the patriarch, had been left in the lurch.

"Why, dear me!" she said. "There is the bell, and we are not nearly through with the lesson." Yet she said it with intense satisfaction in her voice. Has it never been your fortune to meet Sabbath-school teachers who thought if they succeeded in spending the thirty-five minutes allowed them for teaching without getting half through with the lesson, it was proof positive that they were faithful, successful teachers, overflowing with ideas? Such a one was Miss Parkhurst.

Now, what in the name of all that is surprising, was that young lady's motive in coming, with some degree of regularity, week after week, and year after year, to the Harvard Street Sunday school? Various reasons had been given. There were indolent, censorious people who said it was because she liked to show how smart she was in getting up so early; there were vain people who said she wanted one more place in which to exhibit her pretty face and dress; there were gossipy people who said she wanted to get Mr. Robert Hammond to take an interest in her, and that she would find herself disappointed, for she was not by any means one of his sort. I do not know that a single person attributed the right motive to her work.

I do earnestly assure you that it was simply and honestly a desire to be in the right place and do the right thing. Vain she certainly was, to some extent. A great many people are. How else can we account for — well, a great many things? But it had never once occurred to her to choose the Sabbath-school room as a special place in which to exhibit her fair face and fairer robes. She wore her prettiest and brightest. Oh, yes, indeed, there are many who do that same thing; but to teach a class in Sunday school was always considered the right and proper thing to do, and because it *was* right and proper, Miss Parkhurst wanted to do it.

3

WORK THAT COSTS

Mr. Lewis put his boots, with his feet inside them, on the back of the nearest chair and held his cigar in his hand.

"I suppose I mustn't smoke this in here?" he said inquiringly.

Mr. Hammond shook his head with a quiet smile.

"No," he said, "I can't have false witnesses lurking about my rooms."

Mr. Lewis laughed and laid his cigar on the table.

Mr. Hammond went on with the pile of papers he was filing, and his companion watched him in silence for several minutes; then he drew a heavy sigh.

"Satan is at work with all his might this week," he said presently.

"Did you ever know a week in which he wasn't?" Mr. Hammond questioned. "I have often thought that he might be an example of industry and perseverance. Is there anything especially new requiring his skill?"

"Yes, there is. Something that affects our boys."

Mr. Hammond laid down his papers and wheeled around quickly in his chair.

"What is it?" he said, every faculty on the alert.

"Why, there's a miserable — I don't know what you call it — supper and ride, and whatnot, coming off on Thursday evening — gotten up by some of the worst fellows in town, only they have money and a certain degree of position. They are going to finish the evening with cards. It's a trap to get in some more gamblers; and our boys, yours and mine, are invited."

"All my boys?"

"All but young Armstrong. They might as well invite Deacon Mills, as him. Larry Bates is almost one of the ringleaders — he and those academy boys. They're a wild couple, Hammond."

"Who told you about it?"

"Mr. Gordon. His Will is determined to go. Of course he won't give his consent; but he is in great trouble about it. He is afraid Will may take French leave. He says it is very difficult to control him. He thinks he is old enough to be his own master."

"What are you going to do about it?"

"Do? Oh, nothing! There's nothing *I* can

do. My boys will go, to a man. I know they will; the very spirit of evil is in every one of them, anyway. It looks like a hopeless task to stem such a tide of impishness by an hour's work on Sunday."

"It can't be done," Mr. Hammond said emphatically.

"Of course it can't; and yet a man wouldn't feel justified in giving up his class in Sabbath school on that account."

"I should think not! The remedy lies rather in carrying the Sabbath work all through the week with us, in our thoughts and prayers and plans. But about our boys. We must do something."

"I tell you there's nothing to do. We can't command or control them in any way. I did think at one time of taking every one of mine to the concert; but, in the first place, they wouldn't *be* taken — they would rather go to the other affair; and, in the second place, I've got to be out of town myself, on important business."

"And, in the third place, it is Thursday evening, you say. We can't work against our prayer meeting."

"But they won't go to prayer meeting; and they certainly might better be at a concert than at any of these other places. I should feel justified in taking them to any place of interest that I could find; shouldn't you?"

Mr. Hammond shook his head.

"I never like to fight Satan with his own weapons," he said gravely. "He understands everything pertaining to his business so much better than we do. You see, we profess to think the prayer meeting of greater importance than any place of entertainment, and it is necessary that our profession and practice should carefully agree."

"Yes, but see here. You go to the concert for the sake of keeping your boys away from a dangerous place, provided they would give up the other place for you, which they wouldn't; but it seems to me the object would justify the means."

"I shouldn't agree with you. It is, at least, a sort of 'doing evil that good may come,' which is in itself inconsistent. I shouldn't hope to benefit my class by such a proceeding. Boys are sharp fellows. They know when the precept and the practice agree, and when there is a discrepancy."

"Then you think a Christian shouldn't have the prayer meeting under any circumstances whatever?"

Mr. Hammond laughed.

"I certainly didn't mean to say any such

thing," he said pleasantly. "You jump at conclusions. I shall begin to think that you are doubtful of the propriety of *your* being out of town on Thursday evening."

"Well, now, I wonder what you would do in such a case. I'm going out to see Cornelia."

"Is there no other evening that will answer the purpose?"

"Why, she is going to have company. Their meeting is on Wednesday evening. You wouldn't go now, I'll venture."

Mr. Hammond shook his head.

"I cannot say that, positively. I can only say I think I wouldn't. If my sense of duty were as clear under the circumstances as it is now without the circumstances."

"Well," said Mr. Lewis, rising and laughing as he spoke, "my sense of duty is muddled, I presume. Anyway, Cornelia expects me, and I'm not inclined to disappoint her."

After Mr. Lewis's departure, Mr. Hammond sat down in a brown study. He left the bills on the table. He glanced at his watch and at his memorandums, to make sure that no one was waiting at his office by appointment. Then, apparently, he studied the vines on the carpet; at least, he fixed his eyes on them and thought. Presently he got out his writing desk, and, taking the first slip of paper that presented itself, he wrote the following:

WEDNESDAY MORNING

DEAR CLARA:

I can't be present at your dinner party tomorrow. The necessity is upon me to give a party myself; one to which I cannot invite you, either. Woe is me! I will look in during the day, if possible, and explain; also, I will come in tomorrow evening after the meeting. Present my regards to Miss Marion.

As ever,
ROB

Then he selected some of his rarest note-paper and sent a carefully worded note:

CLARENDON HOUSE, JAN. 27, 18—

R. L. Hammond's kind regards to Lawrence Bates and requests the pleasure of his company to dinner on Thursday, the 28th, at 4 o'clock. A carriage will be in readiness to convey Mr. Hammond and his guests to the Harvard Street

Church in time for evening service.

Duplicates of this note were written and addressed to each of his Sabbath scholars. Then Mr. Hammond went down to the office, dispatched a boy with his notes, held a consultation with one of the proprietors, another with the head waiter, and finally made all possible speed to his neglected office. His trap was set, and all he could do was to await results. Yes, there was one other thing to do. Mr. Hammond was a lawyer — a popular one — and business pressed upon him. Several gentlemen were waiting to consult him on important business. Having given due attention to each, and before entering into the regular business of the day, he went into his private office, closed and locked the door, and then and there presented to his Father the request that was at that moment pressing on his heart. That God, in his loving-kindness, would follow the invitations just sent out and incline the hearts of the boys toward their teacher. It is not everyone who, having made arrangements to give a party, goes to his Father in heaven for help and encouragement. It would be a matter of curiosity to follow those notes to their various destinations and discover the reception they met with. Larry Bates and Lester St. John were together, as indeed they were very much given to being. They had been making plans for the next evening when the small messenger from the Clarendon House pounced down upon them.

"Here, you, Larry Bates, I've got something for you; and you, too, for the matter of that." This last in a less familiar tone.

Larry Bates was boon companion with everybody, but Lester St. John was more choice of his acquaintance, as a rule. The two young men stopped in the street and viewed their respective letters in great surprise.

"What's up?" Larry said, in characteristic fashion, and St. John, true to his character, proceeded rapidly to a discovery of the contents.

"Whew!" Larry said, as he looked over his friend's shoulder. "I presume that's what mine is. Ain't that rich? Dinner at the Clarendon House! That's pretty tall, ain't it? It's a regular pity that it comes on Thursday. What's got into everything to pile on top of each other? What do you think of it, Lester?"

"That," said Lester St. John, speaking slowly and with unqualified admiration in his voice, "is what I call sharp."

"Sharp! Why, do you suppose he has heard?"

"Of course he's heard, and he's going to attempt heading us off; and if it hasn't been done smoothly, then I don't know. Here's the academy; let's go in and see if Lew and Arthur have one."

Those two gentlemen were found in their room playing football with their geometry; at least, that is what they had been engaged in before the arrival of the invitation. They received their friends with great eagerness.

"Have you got one? Yes, you have. Then it's just what Lew thought it was, a come around. Who's been and watched what we were doing, I wonder? Well, it's a cute one, and no mistake. Now how'll we answer it? That's the question. St. John, you're an orator; just get us up a smooth and flowing regret, and we can each copy it with a change of adjectives here and there."

It was Arthur Sanford who delivered this eager speech. He was perched on the window seat, his handsome face aglow with fun. He kicked his writing desk, which was on the floor at his feet, toward St. John as he spoke, and added:

"Come, give us a real fine thing, and I'll get a sheet of tinted note paper and copy mine with what variations I need."

Lester St. John composedly took the vacant window seat and answered in his usual tone of composure:

"My answer might not suit you as a copy. I'm not going to send a regret."

"You don't say you are *going?*" This from all three of his hearers in concert. "Why, St. John, how can you? — it's the same night, you know."

"Can't help it. A sleigh ride with a set of loungers and saloon keepers isn't such a wonderful honor. I'm about half sick of this nonsense anyway. You and Lew would get into no end of trouble about it, and Will Gordon would have to run away if he went at all. Now, what's the use? Here comes a first-class invitation from a first-class gentleman, who will do things up in fine style. I think, myself, the fun lies in that direction, and I've decided to go there."

The boys seemed wonderfully astonished, Arthur Sanford a trifle crestfallen.

"Why, I thought you expected rare sport," he said, somewhat crossly.

"Well, as to sport, I'm not so hard up for that sort of thing that I need to find it among that set altogether. Anyhow, when a man like Mr. Hammond gives me a polite invitation, why, I like to accept it, I know enough."

Somebody tore up the stairs, three steps at a time, and Will Gordon burst into the room, puffing and panting in his haste.

"Here you are," he said breathlessly. "I thought I should find you. Now, what's to be done about it all?"

"St. John is going," announced all three of the boys.

Will Gordon looked relieved. Since he could not go to the original entertainment, at least by fair means, he inclined toward the second invitation; and it was evidently an unexpected pleasure to have so powerful an ally as Lester St. John.

"We might go to the dinner, and then leave — have another engagement, you know," Lewis Sanford ventured thoughtfully.

St. John shook his head.

"I shan't go in for *that*," he said with decision. "Not by a long shot. If Mr. Hammond had set a trap for us, inviting us to dinner and saying nothing about the meeting until he got us there — why, then, I'd talk about another engagement as large as anybody; but when he has been open and aboveboard, I'm not going to eat my dinner at his table and then sneak off. He's treated us like gentlemen, and I say, let's be gentlemen with him."

"Then you'd go to the whole thing, prayer meeting and all?" This from Will Gordon, unbounded astonishment in his voice.

"Course I should," said St. John, relishing the wonder that he was exciting. "I ain't afraid of a prayer meeting, I hope. I never could see that they hurt anybody; so, if it will be any comfort to Mr. Hammond to take me there, why, I'm willing to be taken."

Larry Bates had been still a long time for him.

"I'll tell you what we can do to a dot," he said, springing from the woodbox where he had been sitting. "We can go the whole thing, prayer meeting and all, as Lester says, and get back to Allyn Street by quarter past eight — that is time enough for the game; then, you see, we've done the right thing by everybody, and can afford to finish the evening to suit ourselves."

This arrangement met with unqualified approval from all present, and Satan, no doubt, chuckled over Mr. Hammond's defeat. Late in the afternoon of that same day, Mr. Lewis bustled into his friend's office.

"Let me see one of your invitations," he said eagerly. "I've heard about them, you see. Haven't you a copy?"

"I wrote one more than was needed, I found, and I think I have it in my pocket-book."

"Well, now, that's very fine; you did it up in first-class style. I say, Hammond, you think you've done it, don't you?"

"No," said Mr. Hammond with a grave smile. "I only think I've *tried* to do it."

"Suppose you fail?"

"If I *do,* do you think the fault will be mine?"

"No, I *don't.* There's something in that. Well, I can tell you just exactly how far you have succeeded. They are coming to the dinner, and going to the meeting, and after that they are going to the other place to join in a famous game of cards that is to be played for a silver knife that one of the nice young men is to present to the successful party. Isn't that a lovely arrangement, and don't you hope your dinner and your prayer meeting will do them good?"

"They may," Mr. Hammond said quietly. "Where did you gain your information, Lewis?"

"Of my boy, Tony. He is everywhere, and sees everybody, and what Tony doesn't know really isn't worth knowing."

After Mr. Lewis's departure, the lawyer was very busy again — a stream of business set toward his private office, so that one would have thought there was no room for outside matters; but, apparently, he did some thinking not connected with law, for at the earliest opportunity he wrote another note.

EVENING

DEAR CLARA:

I find I cannot be with you after prayer meeting tomorrow. At least, I hope I can't. That sentence needs explaining when I see you. I am full of important business just now. Will give a detailed account of myself on Friday.

Hastily,
ROB

4

WORK FOR ONE DAY

It would have delighted your eyes to have seen the dining table at the Clarendon House after the head waiter had put the finishing touches on its arrangement. It glittered with silver and sparkled with glass, to say nothing of the array of appetizing dishes; in all respects, as fine an entertainment as could have been gotten up for older guests. In Mr. Hammond's rooms everything was bright and cheery. The large, handsome stereoscope was placed in the best light, and the small, marble table on which it stood was strewn with choice photographs; a book of rare engravings of a scientific nature lay in a conspicuous spot for the scientific nature of Lester St. John to delight himself in; a collection of richly colored plates had been brought out with the hope of pleasing the beauty-loving Tom Gordon. Toto, the kitchen parrot, with a chattering tongue, had been borrowed for the occasion, because Mr. Hammond fancied that Larry Bates, and perhaps the Sanfords, might like to cultivate his acquaintance. Not a boy had been forgotten, not an individual taste but had been studied; and at ten minutes of four the host sat in his easy chair, apparently a gentleman of elegant leisure, waiting for his honored guests.

They came in as a body — at least the Sanfords and St. John came together, with Will Gordon bringing up the rear. Larry Bates was half an hour behind time, but he was always that, even when there was to be nothing but fun in prospect. Peter Armstrong was prompt as to time, but came alone, as he usually had to; there was nobody who assimilated with Peter. Poor Job Jenkins could not come at all. His father was indulging in an attack of delirium tremens, and Job was obliged to watch over him; so the only party to which the poor fellow was ever invited was lost to him.

They were a very merry party who sat down to that private dinner table. Mr. Hammond appeared as young as any of them. The boys were perfectly amazed to discover how many games he knew, and how fond he had been of playing them when he was a schoolboy. "Not that he had gotten over his fondness for them either," he said; "only there was very little time in which to indulge his tastes in that line nowadays." They had disposed of oysters and turkey, with their accompaniments, and were eating mince and lemon pie and drinking coffee when Mr. Hammond said:

"By the way, St. John, I thought of you and Gordon today, when I read a certain notice. Did either of you ever hear LeFevre?"

No, they never had.

"Well, you know about him?"

No, they didn't even know about him.

"Ah! then that is better yet. You ought to make his acquaintance. He is one of the most thoroughly scientific scholars in the country, and the most successful experiments in philosophy that we have — some of his experiments — are perfectly wonderful; you would be just delighted to see them. Well, he lectures tonight at Trenton Hall, before the Scientific Association. Now, I have a brilliant plan. It isn't more than a mile from Harvard Street Church to Trenton Hall. Our prayer meeting closes at eight, and the lecture commences at eight. I have secured some pretty fast horses for the evening, and with some rapid driving we should reach there before Professor LeFevre has had time to say much. What do you all say to making the attempt?"

"But the Scientific Association is a private affair," St. John said, speaking with breathless eagerness. "None but members are allowed to attend the lectures, and the advanced class are the only students who are members. What good will it do us?"

"I've thought of all that," Mr. Hammond said, smiling. "President Chapin is a particular friend of mine, and I so represented my needs to him as to secure tickets for every one of us; shall we go?"

There were several points of interest in all this, of which Mr. Hammond was aware. In the first place, anything like a philosophical experiment was an absolute passion with Lester St. John — and Will Gordon, though not quite so wild on the subject, was still intensely interested. In the second place, the Scientific Association was a clique by itself; a company of wealthy, cultured, intensely selfish people, who enjoyed what others could not secure, and what, with the perversity common to human nature, others were very eager to secure because they couldn't. The Sanfords understood this perfectly. To be admitted into the charmed circle of the Scientific Association, to be among the privileged few who trod the carpeted aisles and occupied the velvet-cushioned seats of Trenton Hall, an elegant room gotten up by and appropriated to the special use of these intellectual gourmands, to penetrate where some of the academy boys were actually quivering to go, where even Professor Stuart, the head teacher at the academy, was excluded, *this* triumph the Sanfords could appreciate. As for St. John, his eyes fairly glowed with pleasure. The game of cards, with which the evening was to have been finished, passed utterly from his mind, and he said, eagerly: "It is the one place where I have longed to get and couldn't. Father might have been a member if he had chosen; he was invited, but he wouldn't join. He said the expense was enormous, and it wouldn't pay. He don't care for scientific lectures. Are you a member, Mr. Hammond?"

Mr. Hammond bowed. "I was one of the original founders. Although the society has taken a different form from what I had ever supposed it would, and one that I do not approve — it is altogether too selfish a way of enjoying one's self — however, the enjoyment is very fine. Well, shall we all go?"

"Wouldn't you like to?" St. John said eagerly, appealing to the Sanfords.

"Yes, we would," Lewis said, "if for no other reason than because that tiresome

Hick Williams is always telling that his brother-in-law, Justyn Matthews, was invited to join the association and has been to two entertainments at Trenton Hall. He thinks he's something wonderful because his brother-in-law has been invited. What will he say to our going, do you suppose? Won't that be jolly, Arthur?"

I hope Mr. Hammond was gratified with the motive that these young gentlemen had for being pleased, but it was better than playing cards in that low saloon. Good-natured Larry Bates was indifferent alike to science and aristocracy, though he admitted that he liked experiments well enough when they went right; but he was thoroughly good-natured and willing to be led by the latest idea that happened to be suggested to him, so he made no objection to the change of program. Peter Armstrong was secretly as much delighted as St. John could possibly be. He knew very little about philosophy, but he liked to know about everything that could be learned.

"Do they really never receive anyone into the association on his own request?" St. John questioned as they left the dinner table.

"Never," Mr. Hammond said, "unless he has been previously voted in by all the members. They are very particular, but they have some good rules. They never vote on anybody who uses liquor or who plays cards. However, that is not strange; gentlemen of scientific tastes and acquirements never indulge in those follies, as a rule."

St. John and Will Gordon exchanged lightning glances. They were glad that that game of cards was not played. They were both inclined to be gentlemen of scientific tastes. Very little was talked of between this and seven o'clock but Professor LeFevre and his wonderful experiments, about which Mr. Hammond was well-posted; and a very well satisfied company stowed themselves away in the handsome carriage and were whirled toward Harvard Street Church.

Now, this prayer meeting was one that had been much on Mr. Hammond's heart since he had determined on his invitations. He had made it a matter of earnest prayer. I cannot say that it had been believing prayer, because, in that case, he would have been *expecting* results, instead of dimly hoping for them. How little praying in faith there is in this world, anyway. Have we not, many of us, prayed much and often for some blessing, and been overwhelmed with astonishment when our prayers were answered? It was somewhat after this fashion that Mr. Hammond had prayed for the prayer meeting. Harvard Street Church was one of the places that is never very light, nor in cold weather very warm; but the mild evening was favorable, and one can turn on the gas promptly.

Mr. Hammond availed himself of this privilege, after he had seated the boys to their satisfaction. The attendance was unusually large, owing to the mildness and the moonlight. The singing was done with spirit, Mr. Hammond, who was very often the impromptu leader on prayer-meeting evenings, taking care to select tunes that were entirely familiar.

Mr. Gordon read the customary half-dozen verses and offered prayer, then singing, and Mr. Hammond prayed, so did Judge Evans and Mr. Grey; then singing again, and Mr. Hammond spoke a few earnest words, and then the spirit of dumbness took possession of the congregation.

In vain Mr. Gordon said, "The meeting is yours, brethren," and again in pleading tones, "I hope the brethren will not allow the time to run to waste." There the brethren sat in solemn silence. Mr. Hammond turned the leaves of his hymnbook nervously. It seemed hardly proper to sing again, and yet continuous singing was surely better than doing nothing. Another verse was sung — an appropriate selection:

> *"Must Jesus bear the cross alone,*
> *And all the world go free?*
> *No, there's a cross for everyone,*
> *And there's a cross for me."*

"Not a very heavy one," Mr. Gordon said gently. "Surely it is not a hard thing here in this quiet room to speak a word for the Master. Is there no one to witness for him tonight?"

Not a word said anybody. The iron pillars, whose business it was to support the visible building, could not have been more immovable than were the flesh and blood pillars sitting solemnly in their seats. And there sat six boys looking eagerly on. In five of them, at least, the spirit of fun was rampant. There sat their Sabbath-school teacher, who, with infinite trouble and no little expense, had gathered them all into the prayer meeting for the first time in their lives. He had good reason to fear that they would never voluntarily come again. How that meeting dragged! Never was so much singing done in the space of three-quarters of an hour in any meeting not especially devoted to song; never was it more manifestly done for the purpose of taking up the time.

"Well," Mr. Gordon said at last, "if no one has anything to say, we will close the meeting," and the benediction was immediately pronounced.

"My!" Arthur Sanford said, shrugging his shoulders, when they were seated in the carriage. "If the boys should go to recitations no better primed than they were at that meeting this evening, the professor would send them back to get their lessons, wouldn't he, Lew?"

"Mr. Hammond," chimed in Larry Bates, "do folks go to that meeting because they want to, or because they think they must, or *what* is it? It's an awful dull place, anyhow; don't you think so?"

"Prayer meetings are queer institutions," Lester St. John said. "They always seemed to me like the Roman Catholics."

"Like the Roman Catholics!" Will Gordon said. "Why? How?"

"Like their penances and fast days, and things of that sort. Is there something meritorious about it, Mr. Hammond? Do they expect to have it charged to their account?"

There was intense, though good-natured, sarcasm in Lester St. John's face and voice, and Mr. Hammond's heart was heavy within him. How strange the testimony of the witnesses had been that evening! It was well for Mr. Hammond's scheme that Professor LeFevre was in town. From such a meeting, the boys would have gone back with much glee to their cards, and probably given to an admiring audience an account of the degree of interest that had been manifested; but Trenton Hall was a blaze of light, and the elegant audience gathered there was interesting to look upon, and Professor LeFevre's lecture was delightful beyond all description. Even Larry Bates was interested to such an unusual degree that he wrote no notes and ate no peanuts.

"I shall see my guests to their respective homes," Mr. Hammond said as the carriage rolled into Harvard Street.

Will Gordon and Lester St. John protested that they could walk as well as not, but Mr. Hammond urged his courtesy upon them, feeling anxious that no tempting saloon should open its friendly doors for them that evening.

"We have had a capital evening," St. John said, as he was set down at his own home. "I never heard anything so interesting as that lecture. I can't thank you enough for getting us in."

"After all, it was only for one evening. They have escaped once; but there are other evenings to come." This was what his friend, Mr. Lewis, said to Mr. Hammond the next day, when an account had been given of the evening's work.

"I know that," Mr. Hammond said thoughtfully. "But we only have to meet one evening at a time, you know. Then there are other ways of disposing of other things. I am glad to have saved them from one evening's temptation."

"Of course; but I tell you *what*, Hammond, it must have been pretty expensive business. What did it cost you now, all told?"

"About twenty dollars," Mr. Hammond answered promptly as if that matter had been carefully studied out beforehand.

"Well, now, you see some of us could not have afforded to do it, however good our intentions might have been."

"That is true; every teacher could not afford it, and every teacher has not my peculiar class of boys to deal with; but there are other and less expensive ways to accomplish the same result, probably. I could not afford such an expenditure very *often;* but then you know, Lewis, I don't smoke."

Mr. Lewis laughed. "What has that to do with it? Oh, expense! Pooh! Smoking doesn't cost much; not the way *I* smoke, at least."

Mr. Hammond arched his eyebrows slightly. "Use your knowledge of arithmetic," he said, pushing pencil and paper toward his guest. "Four cigars a day, and that's *exceedingly* moderate, more moderate than you often are, three hundred and sixty-five days in a year, say five cents apiece for convenience, though they cost more; what is the sum?"

"What a horribly methodical fellow you are, Hammond! Four times five is twenty, twice five is ten, twice six, thirteen, twice two — Robinson Crusoe! Who would have imagined it? Several turkeys and carriages all gone to smoke! Well, I *declare* I never thought I spent so much. What mean things figures are! Sour, snarly, matter-of-fact creatures. What about the prayer meeting, Hammond?"

Mr. Hammond's face clouded. "It was the only thing that failed," he said sadly. "I am not surprised that people not governed by Christian principle are repelled from such meetings."

"Surprised!" Mr. Lewis said heartily; "Why *should* you be? Did you ever know a greater misnomer than calling them *social* prayer meetings? I defy anyone to get up any idea of sociability in connection with our gatherings of that name. I tell you, Hammond, religion has been frozen and choked and *smothered* in that room, just according to the season of the year."

5

WORK THAT PUZZLES

Miss Parkhurst's class was in a giggle. That isn't a very smooth-sounding word, but that exactly describes their condition. The time was the usual session of Sabbath school, and the occasion was a gentleman who had been invited to speak a few words to the school. Now, that gentleman was dressed in a very quiet suit of gray cloth. He had an unfashionable way of combing his hair. He had a nervous way of winding his pocket handkerchief around one hand when he spoke. He had a somewhat unpleasant voice. As an offset to these immense disadvantages, he had some very earnest, solemn words to speak to both teachers and scholars. Most of the school listened decorously. Those who were too indifferent to the subject before them to be interested were courteous enough to hear, even though their thoughts were off on a tangent. But Miss Parkhurst's class must be considered an exception. They were very far from being interested. They made no attempt to conceal their amusement. By some strange combination of circumstances, the stray sheep whose nominal fold was in that corner were all present on this particular occasion, which was unfortunate for the gentleman in question.

Miss Evans rustled her silken robes and tapped with the toe of her gaiter on the floor, and occasionally, between the turning of the hymnbook leaves with a rattling sound, laughed outright at some comment which her friend, Fanny Horton, whispered in her ear.

"He dyes his whiskers, I do believe," murmured May Horton, on the other side. "And they are one-sided, too. He evidently gets his wife to trim them."

"I don't believe he *has* a wife," said Miss Evans. "If he had, she would tell him not to attempt public speaking. Miss Parkhurst, is the interesting gentleman who is holding forth a married man?"

"I'm sure I don't know," Miss Parkhurst said, smiling roguishly. "I might ascertain if you are particularly desirous of knowing; but isn't he rather *old*, Celia?"

This question drew such bursts of half-suppressed merriment from the three young ladies that Mr. Hammond turned in his seat and fixed a stern gaze on them.

"Do look at Mr. Hammond," whispered

Fanny Horton. "He looks like the statue of Fate in the reading room. Girls, do hush. I'm half afraid he will call us by name, as they do the children in Miss Holmes's class."

"I would advise him not to try it," answered Miss Celia, with darkening brows. "He owns most everybody and manages nearly everything, but I still recognize my right to breathe without his permission."

Miss Sarah Blake took up the conversation:

"Miss Parkhurst, where did that man come from? I wonder if he is going to talk all day. *I* want to get home to my dinner. Sunday is the only day I have time to eat anything, and he is going to cheat me out of that."

The trio at the end of the seat shook with laughter, partly at the speaker's expense, partly at Sarah's. Miss Parkhurst responded sweetly:

"I don't know who he is, I am sure. Someone that our superintendent picked up somewhere, I presume. You know he has talents in that direction. The gentleman has a singular way of combing his hair, hasn't he?"

"I should think he has!" exclaimed Fanny Horton. "It looks as though there might have been a piece of Alcock's porous plaster stuck on at each side."

"His voice is the worst part of him," Miss Celia said. "It cuts through my head like a knife. Miss Parkhurst, why do they allow every old stick that comes along to practice his powers of speech on us?"

Miss Parkhurst laughed. "I'm sure I don't know," she said pleasantly, "unless it is to teach us the virtue of patient endurance. I have no doubt, though, that what he is saying is very good. Hatty seems to be interested."

Miss May Horton's lip curled. "That is an undoubted evidence of its excellence, of *course*, especially of its intellectual worth," she said, with such pointed sarcasm in tone that Miss Parkhurst shook her head warningly; but Hatty Taylor apparently neither heard nor saw. She had moved a little apart from the others, had gathered her plain, neat calico dress into as close a compass as she could, and sat with her great gray eyes fixed steadily on the speaker, while the glow on her cheek and the utter quietude of her entire form bespoke rapt attention. She gave a little sigh, as of one let down from some height, when the speaker suddenly ceased, and turning her earnest face to Miss Parkhurst, said simply:

"Wasn't it splendid?"

Whereupon the entire class, Sarah Blake included, laughed outright.

"There are various degrees of taste and enjoyment, are there not, Miss Parkhurst?" Miss Evans said. "And intellect," she added, in lower tones.

"Oh, yes," Miss Parkhurst answered, "and it is very fortunate that it is so."

Then to Hatty, in kindly tone:

"I am glad you enjoyed it, Hatty. I think the poor man must be very grateful to you for giving him your undivided attention. I'm afraid the rest of us were not so helpful."

"If I believed a word he said, I think very likely it would have been interesting to me, but I don't."

This Sarah Blake said, emphatically. Miss Parkhurst smiled on her and shook her head. "I am afraid you are a sad skeptic, Sarah," she said sweetly.

"If I had heard a word he said," Miss Fanny Horton yawned, "I think very likely I might have believed it. Girls, isn't it blessed that he has got through?"

And then these young ladies arose and sang, in rich, clear voices:

"Living for Jesus, only for Jesus,
Striving in wisdom, daily we grow."

69

"There are the Marcys in Sunday school," whispered Celia Evans, pausing in the midst of the words, " 'Wondrous love of Jesus,' " to say it. "What has happened to them? They never stayed before, did they? Did you know they were here? Augusta and Loraine are both here, and their brother Elbert. I didn't know he was at home." Then she took up the refrain again, " 'Oh, the love of Jesus.' "

In the hum of voices that followed the superintendent's dismissal came many words that puzzled Miss Parkhurst's class. "How does he happen to be here?" "Why, he is a friend of Elbert Marcy, and he coaxed him home with him for a visit." "He's going to speak tonight." "Oh, is he?" "Yes, they are going to secure the hall for him. They say no church will hold the throng when it gets out who is here."

"Who in the world are they all buzzing about?" Celia Evans said. "I haven't seen anybody wonderful, have you, Fan?"

Then came the singular voice that had so disturbed her brain, speaking right behind her:

"There is one young lady in this class, Marcy, to whom I want an introduction. I want to thank her. Her earnest eyes fixed steadily on mine helped me immensely."

"In *this class?*" answered Mr. Elbert Marcy's stately tones. "I observed them. I thought they were anything but helpful, or even respectable."

"There was one exception. That lady at the end."

"Miss Taylor," Mr. Marcy said, raising his voice, "step this way, won't you? My friend, Dr. Millington, would like to speak to you."

Dr. Millington! Miss Evans looked from Fanny to May Morton, and all were speechless. Greater even than the stinging rebuke coming from General Marcy's son was the rebuke and the bewilderment of this name, a name over which the literary world was aglow; a name that was better and more widely known, perhaps, than that of any other in the country; as belonging alike to a scholar, a traveler, a philanthropist, and a brilliant lecturer; a name that Miss Evans had spoken of in a gush of eager enthusiasm not long ago to Mr. Marcy himself.

"She would give more to see and hear Dr. Millington for five minutes," she had said, "than any, yes, than *all* other great men combined." She distinctly remembered saying so; and here he was just behind her, shaking hands with Hatty Taylor, the factory girl! Actually thanking her for helping him by her undivided attention!

Miss Parkhurst maintained her composure. "I thought there was something striking in his appearance," she said to Miss Raymer. "But I'm so tired today that I really don't know what he said. I was out late last evening." Then she rustled herself to Mr. Hammond's side of the room. She had a pet scheme under way. "I want your help in a plan which is entirely after your own heart," she said to him, with a winning smile. "I heard glowing accounts of the elegant dinner party that you gave your class last week. I can't resist the temptation of telling you that I do so admire your self-denying efforts to entertain them socially."

"I beg your pardon," interrupted Mr. Hammond. "St. John, may I trouble you to ask Brother Newton to wait for me a few minutes?" And Mr. Hammond looked relieved as St. John moved away. It did not suit his taste, nor his plans, to have it reported among his boys that he denied himself to entertain them.

Miss Parkhurst continued. "And I really must thank you for the inspiration — it has given me an idea. I'm going to get my class together at my own house — just a little informal company. I've invited your class also. I thought it might be pleasant for them to meet each other. Now, I have a special favor to ask of you. Won't you come in on Tuesday evening and help entertain them? You understand the art so well — I know you must — for you succeed so beautifully with those boys. Can I depend on you? Just for a little while, you know."

"Tuesday evening!" said Mr. Hammond, inquiringly. "Why, that is prayer-meeting evening, you know!"

"Oh, why so it is; but then — Mr. Hammond, do you really succeed in attending both prayer meetings? I have been obliged to give up the Tuesday meetings altogether. My engagements are such that I really haven't time for them."

"I cannot always attend," said Mr. Hammond. "But your young ladies, Miss Parkhurst? The meeting is designed more especially for the young people, you know."

"Oh, my girls never attend it — never — so that will not be in the way at all."

"But you try to induce them to attend it?"

"Why, no; as to that, I never thought of it. Besides, they wouldn't go if I did; they every one of them do *exactly* as they please, without any reference to me. I don't know but Hatty Taylor attends them. I never heard her say so, but it would be quite like her. However, she won't mind missing one evening."

Mr. Hammond shook his head. "There is a boy in my class who, I am sure, would object to giving up the meeting, even for one evening; and I'm trying to induce all my boys to attend it."

"But they have all accepted my invitation, except that Peter Armstrong; and he is so queer I don't suppose he would enjoy it if he came. Just for this once, Mr. Hammond."

"I must still beg to be excused," he said earnestly. "I have long made it a very earnest rule to form *no* engagements of a social or a business nature on evenings set apart by the church to prayer; it would have to be an *exceedingly* important matter that would lead me to violate that rule. I preach consistency to my class, and I must make my theory and practice agree."

"But, after all, Mr. Hammond, isn't there such a thing as being *too* particular? The girls in my class are not Christians at all. Mercy! They are far enough from being such. Isn't there danger of disgusting them with the subject by being too strict and formal in our lives?"

Mr. Hammond smiled sadly. "Did you ever observe," he asked, "how keen those persons who are not Christians at all are to discover and comment on the shortcomings and inconsistencies of others? Especially is it the case with young ladies and gentlemen of the stamp that compose your and my classes. I am often in fear lest some lapse of mine may cause them to think lightly of my profession. I hardly think I *can* be *too* careful."

Miss Parkhurst sighed, heavily. "Dear me!" she said. "If you live in fear lest you may not do just right, I don't know what is to become of those poor sinners who only do right once in a while. Well, I suppose I must select some other evening; though, really, I can't see how I can. Surely I can't miss Mrs. Monroe's reception on Wednesday evening. Do you go to that, Mr. Hammond? No? Why, I'm shocked at you! Do you really intend to give up all recreation in that way? I think you owe some duties to society. Just put it in that light, and I'm sure we shall see you more often. You are so fond of the word *duty*. Do you really think there is something in it?"

"There is a great deal in it," Mr. Hammond replied, smiling over the progress they made. "But our conceptions of the subject might be different and involve more time for discussion than we have to spare;" then in a louder tone — "Don't let me detain you, Brother Newton."

"I'm detaining you," Miss Parkhurst said hurriedly. "I'm shocked at having kept you so; just help me out of my dilemma, and I will vanish. Monday evening my friend, Miss Hinckley, has a social gathering. Monday is a very strange evening for tea parties. Don't you think so? Well, that disposes of *that* evening. Wednesday is Mrs. Monroe's reception, as I said. Thursday is the church prayer meeting. I suppose it would be no better to have it then than on Tuesday. In fact, I don't like to have to go to other places *myself* on Thursday evenings. Well, could you give us *Friday* evening? I *was* going into town, but I suppose I *can* give it up."

Mr. Hammond laughed. "Teachers' meeting," he said briefly.

Miss Parkhurst shrugged her handsome shoulders. "You see how it is," she said, an undertone of impatience in her words. "There *really* isn't any evening *but* Tuesday."

"And there *certainly* isn't that," he said, with quiet positiveness.

"Then we shall just have to say Saturday.

I don't like that evening at all, because one always sleeps later on Sunday mornings *anyway* than any other time, and after having company, one's house is always in such confusion, but that is part of the sacrifice for our work. Well, say Saturday evening, then. At what hour may we expect you?"

Mr. Hammond hesitated — *he* did not like Saturday evening, for the reason that it had been one of the standing rules of his Christian life not to break the Sabbath on Saturday; but Miss Parkhurst evidently considered herself as doing a meritorious thing in sacrificing herself, perhaps he ought to be sacrificed also. Besides, it was growing late. His Sabbath-afternoon work waited. So he promised.

6

WORK THAT IS TANGLED

It wanted but fifteen minutes to nine o'clock when Mr. Hammond rang sharply at Miss Parkhurst's door.

"I owe you an apology," he said to that lady, who came to the hall to welcome him. "I had no idea of being detained so late by important business, or I should have sent you word. In fact, I was amazed at the lateness of the hour and have only come in to bring my regrets. I suppose your pleasant little gathering is nearly over?"

"You shall come in and see for yourself how much we look like breaking up," the lady said, her eyes beaming with pleasure. "We have no idea of returning to primitive regulations in regard to hours. Why, we do not have refreshments until nine."

Mr. Hammond's face clouded slightly. Refreshments at nine! At what hour would these two Sabbath-school classes be likely to go to rest, and in what probable condition of mind and body would the Sabbath morning find them? He followed his hostess into the brightly lighted parlors and rubbed his eyes in a half Rip Van Winkle fashion as he looked about him. He was but slightly acquainted with the young ladies who composed Miss Parkhurst's class, and the transforming effects of tarletan and sashes and flowers and gloves were but little understood by him.

Miss Evans he positively did not recognize. How should he? She was a moving mass of creamy white puffs and blue sash, and tier upon tier of bewildering curls. Moreover, the puffs and curls were in a flutter of excitement, for at the moment of his entrance she was dancing with Lester St. John. Two other young ladies were on the floor with their respective partners, Larry Bates and Will Gordon. There was nothing that Will Gordon was not prepared to do. A little group over by the center table also attracted his gaze. The brothers Sanford were there, engaged in instructing Miss Bates in the art of playing parlor croquet. Over by the window sat Peter Armstrong, alone, alternately looking at the two merry groups and then out on the moonlit lawn. Job Jenkins was not there at all.

Mr. Hammond was no Rip Van Winkle in perception. It took him a few seconds of time to discover that he was in very bewildering circumstances. It was nine o'clock on a Saturday evening, and Miss Parkhurst and he were evidently sacrificing themselves to a croquet and dancing party, which was but just getting into full tide of operation. Both dancers and croquet players halted barely long enough to respond in a general way to his introduction, and then went merrily on.

"Aren't they having a delightful time?" Miss Parkhurst said, with beaming face. "It is really worth the sacrifice of a good deal of time and strength just to see how entirely the young people enjoy it. They enter so heartily into their pleasure."

Perhaps the most ludicrous phase of this entertainment was Miss Parkhurst's utter unconsciousness of anything verging on impropriety. Mr. Hammond studied her face closely and felt that she was innocent of any design to impose upon him and was honestly and simply bent on giving her class a good time. This only made things more perplexing.

"Where is Miss Taylor?" he said, by way of giving time for thought. "I do not see her here."

Miss Parkhurst sighed.

"She is not here, Mr. Hammond. It is

80

strange how one is trammeled in one's efforts to do good. Now one of my plans was to make a nice time for Hatty Taylor, she so seldom has any pleasure. They are quite poor, you know, and don't you think I couldn't prevail on her to come?"

"What excuse did she offer?"

"Oh, the old trouble that meets one at every turn — not at home among the girls. Some of them feel above her, she thinks."

"But isn't there force in the excuse? *Would* she be apt to feel at home? I don't pretend to understand this question of dress. It is rather intricate. But would there not be a marked difference between her toilet and that of the other young ladies?"

"Why, of course she can't dress like Celia Evans or Fanny and May Horton, and certainly in her circumstances ought not to expect to. But what *difference* does it make? Did she think I invited her here to show her dress?"

"Yet, isn't it natural that she should think that from coming in contact with young ladies of her own age looking so utterly unlike her in their attire?"

Miss Parkhurst looked puzzled.

"Perhaps so," she said slowly. "But what are we to do? Isn't that a feeling of false pride?"

"Very likely. Do you consider Miss Taylor's advantages of brain and heart education to have been so superior that she should be able to rise above all feelings of false pride?"

The puzzled look deepened.

"Why, I don't know. Oh, of course not. But then, Mr. Hammond, what are we to do? How can we ever bring our classes together socially if this thing is to spring up between them?"

"I do not know. So long as the present fashion of toilets obtains, it is certainly a very bewildering question. Under the circumstances, I do not see how they can possibly come together with anything like a feeling of ease and pleasure."

"I don't think it would have been any more soothing to her feelings if the girls had all worn calico dresses, out of consideration for her having nothing better. In fact, I think it would be positively rude to make so pointed a matter of her circumstances."

"You mean, I suppose, had they made the change for simply this occasion. I quite agree with you. A sensitive girl would have been wounded instead of helped."

"Mr. Hammond, you can't *possibly* think that all these girls ought to dress in calico all the time because Hatty Taylor can not afford better?"

"I didn't *say* anything of the kind," he answered, smiling. "But, now that you have suggested it, that would certainly settle the vexed question for us, would it not?"

"I should think it would," she said, half breathlessly. "But it is settled in an impossible way. How could it ever be brought about?"

"I don't know. I should think the spirit of it might be accomplished, perhaps, by a very careful study of one sentence in an old book of etiquette, of which I am quite fond."

"Then tell me what the sentence is, for I am really in a great bewilderment. If it is but one sentence, I'm sure I can bring my brains to make so much effort, and I'll engage to study it carefully."

"Will you?" he said, with quiet meaning. Then he repeated, slowly and earnestly: "Whether therefore ye eat, or drink, or whatsoever ye do, do *all* to the glory of God."

It was an entirely grave face and thoughtful eyes that Miss Parkhurst lifted to meet his, as she said:

"Do you *really* think that means such a small thing as dress?"

"Is it *dress* that makes the trouble in your class, or is it 'eating and drinking'? Besides, don't you remember the 'whatsoever'?"

"But, Mr. Hammond, how many people in this world do you suppose make their toilets according to that idea?"

"I really do not know. I know *one* lady who is going to study the idea carefully, and I expect enlightenment."

Miss Parkhurst laughed her sweet, silvery laugh and went to answer a call from the piano.

Meantime, Mr. Hammond's questions remained unsolved. Here he certainly was countenancing and encouraging a dancing party. It really could be nothing less, for the dancing had gone steadily on; so also had the croquet. The main question was what to do. He could go quietly away after an indefinite noncommittal word of apology to Miss Parkhurst. Most of the company were too busy to notice or care for his exit. What a comfort this quiet slipping out of responsibility would be! Why not? Who would be hurt, or helped either, for the matter of that? How much of a stand would that be to take? Given that slippery method of dealing with troublesome questions, how much better or wiser would the world grow? Well, there was another way: He could openly and boldly declare his disapproval of the nature and time of the entertainment, and so depart with his colors flying. What then? Why, then he would succeed in offending Miss Parkhurst and either amusing or startling her guests, according to their several temperaments; but it was doubtful whether he or anyone would be helped thereby. Miss Parkhurst had certainly placed him in a very disagreeable position, but he was nearer to feeling an interest in her than he had been before, for he had discovered that her inconsistencies were the result of thoughtlessness, instead of indifference. Much as these two terms sound alike, there is a marked difference between them. Miss Parkhurst was utterly thoughtless, but her fellow teacher had discovered that evening that she was not utterly indifferent. He finally went over to Peter Armstrong's window. Perhaps the moonlight or some other influence had illuminated Peter, and he might gain an idea.

"Are you enjoying the dancing?" This he asked by way of commending a conversation and was hardly prepared for the quick and emphatic "No, sir," and the look on Peter's face was unmistakable.

"Don't you like to see dancing?"

"No, sir," again said Peter, infinite disgust in his voice. "No, sir, I *don't,* and if I'd known they was going to have that going on tonight, why, I'd have stayed away, that's all. I've had just as much of that kind of thing as I can stand for a spell."

Now this outburst was very unlike quiet, reserved Peter, and Mr. Hammond drew a chair beside him in both amusement and perplexity.

"Where have you been seeing this sort of amusement, my boy? I didn't know you came in contact with it very often."

"No more I don't, and don't want to. That girl did enough of it to last me for a good while."

"What girl?" asked Mr. Hammond, more and more startled.

"Why, that girl that went and danced for her father, and he was silly enough to promise her whatever she wanted, and she went and got John's head. Just think of that! I reckon his disciples didn't ever want to see dancing again. No more do I."

What a sudden transit from the parlors of Miss Parkhurst's elegant home to the court of that Eastern monarch! Yet the law of association had taken the Sabbath-school scholar there and linked the two places. What if those young ladies and gentlemen whizzing around the room could suddenly be confronted with John the Baptist's head on a platter?

"You have been studying your lesson, I fancy," Mr. Hammond said in answer.

"Yes, sir. I wonder now if *they* have?" inclining his head toward the dancers.

"Probably not," his teacher said, smiling over the thought. None of them belonged to the class of people who bestowed much time or thought on Sabbath-school lessons.

"Anyhow, they know about the calf," Peter said again. "We had him quite a spell ago, and he wasn't much more than made before the folks went to dancing around him. I wonder Lester St. John don't think of *them*. He made lots of fun of them."

Mr. Hammond, not finding Peter's views very helpful in regard to his own dilemma, set about trying to puzzle him.

"But the Bible speaks of other kinds of dancing. Did you ever happen to read about a certain Miriam who danced?"

"Yes," said Peter, significantly, "I have; and she sang a psalm at the same time, and, according to my notion, her psalm wouldn't fit in with them folk's dancing over there any better than it would when that girl danced for her father. Besides, I don't believe Miriam whirled around with Moses like Fanny Horton is doing with Will Gordon."

Mr. Hammond could not restrain a laugh. This mode of arguing about the modern question of parlor dancing was so thoroughly unique.

"What about croquet?" he presently asked. "Miss Blake seems to be enjoying the game, and the boys are very patient in their teaching. Why haven't you joined them?"

Peter's honest face grew red and troubled.

"I don't quite know about them," he said earnestly. "I was waiting for you to come so I could speak to you about it. Them red and yellow balls look nice, and I'm most sure I could strike them through those little wires, if that's what they're after; but —"

"Well?" his teacher said, in kindly inquiry.

"Why, they look so exactly like them billiard things that they play with down at the saloon. Tom Randolph took me in one day. He plays there a good deal, and if them things are wrong, why ain't these?"

"But it isn't the red and yellow balls that

are at fault, you know. It is the association. Billiard playing is generally done for money, and croquet is simply for pleasure and exercise. Isn't there a difference?"

"Yes," said Peter, slowly and thoughtfully, "there's a difference. I see that. And there's a difference between drinking a glass of sweet cider in the kitchen at home and going up to the bar and calling for a glass of whiskey. But I don't drink that sweet cider because it don't look fair and square, and real good men who know a great deal don't think it is right; and I can't quite make Tom Randolph see the difference about them billiard things, either. He said his sister, Mrs. Monroe, and her husband and the girls play billiards in their parlor at home, with little balls and little hammers, and he hasn't the time to spare at home, so he comes upstairs to the saloon when he has a few minutes and plays with big balls and a big hammer. He says he only plays for fun, not for money, and he *won't* see any difference. And then the Bible says, you know, 'Abstain from all appearance of evil.' That's the verse on our pledge card, and putting that and Tom Randolph and them things over there together, I can't quite make it out. So I thought I'd wait and ask you. I'd like to play them well enough, but I don't care about having Tom Randolph saying that it's all the same thing, because even if it *isn't,* and he thinks it is, why, then there's an *appearance* of evil, isn't there?"

"It looks like it," said Mr. Hammond, feeling that his bewilderment wasn't lessening. "But, Peter, some people talk just for the sake of hearing themselves talk, you know. What if this Tom Randolph sees the difference plainly enough but doesn't *choose* to admit it?"

"Well, even then," Peter said, with hesitation and embarrassment, "I don't know as I understand about this kind of thing. But wouldn't them balls be an 'occasion for stumbling'?"

"Peter," said Mr. Hammond suddenly, "how long have you owned a Bible?"

"About three months," said wondering Peter.

"Then how have you possibly contrived to become familiar with so many verses?"

"Why," said his scholar in undisguised amazement, "I only know ninety-one — a verse for every day — besides the Sunday-school lesson. Of *course* I learn that."

"Keep on the safe side of these questions, on the Bible side, for the present, my boy. I will give you a general rule which I have found a great benefit in my Christian life. If you find there is the least doubt in your heart as to the right or wrong of a certain path, give Christ the benefit of the doubt, and you will surely be right. Is that clear?"

Then he turned and spoke a word to Miss Parkhurst's young sister, who was presiding at the piano. The music suddenly ceased, and the dancers halted in amazement, waiting further developments. Mr. Hammond stepped forward. His plans were formed. Peter and some of the ninety-one verses had thrown light on the darkness.

7

WORKING IN A STRANGE PLACE

"I owe you an apology," Mr. Hammond said, as he stepped forward, "for bringing your music to a sudden rest; but the fact is, it is growing late on Saturday evening, and I am in some haste. I have been detained from your gathering until this late hour and am only here now to wish you good evening and extend to you an invitation. I have a friend who is very much interested in Sabbath schools, and he is particularly interested, Miss Parkhurst, in our two classes. He has given me leave to invite you all to an entertainment, which he feels very certain that you will enjoy, and I take great pleasure in repeating his message."

Not only the dancing, but the croquet game had ceased with the music, and the entire party were evidently interested in this new development. Miss Evans spoke first, as she was apt to do:

"What sort of an entertainment is it to be — musical, or what?"

"That question is rather broad," Mr.

Hammond said, smiling. "I know there is to be some very fine music. An exceedingly rare treat in that line is expected, but I don't think the program is to be confined to music. In fact, my friend's preparations are on such an unusually grand scale that it is rather difficult to give you a program."

"Is there to be a large party?" Lester St. John asked, with an unusual appearance of interest. He was exceedingly fond of good music.

"A *very* large company, and some very distinguished guests. Some that you will especially enjoy meeting, Will."

"Scientific people?" Will Gordon said, with a lighting up of his handsome eyes.

"Scientists of the very grandest attainments. Some of them are special friends of his, and there is one exceedingly eminent historian."

Arthur Sanford shrugged his shoulders a little.

"I am afraid it is a literary entertainment," he said laughingly, "and I would be ridiculously out of place in such a gathering. I go in for fun."

"It is the best place I have ever heard of in which to enjoy one's self," Mr. Hammond said, heartily. "Sanford, I'll ensure you a good time if you go."

"Oh, I'll go, I presume. I always try every sort of amusement I can find. There is none too much to be had in this world."

"Mr. Hammond, will your friend allow dancing?" Sarah Blake said, mischief sparkling in her eyes.

"From your tone and manner, Miss Sarah, I infer that you consider it very doubtful. May I ask you why?"

"Oh, scientific gentlemen are not given to that sort of thing, are they?"

"Scientific people, scholarly people, musical people, and dancing people do not match. Is that the idea?"

"Well, something like that, I suppose. I mean —" Sarah said, slightly abashed.

"It has never occurred to me to class dancing among the entertainments of that occasion; but we might make inquiries in regard to the probabilities, if it is likely to be an important omission."

"I presume we could all survive without that employment," Lester St. John said, a little haughtily.

The half mocking tone in which Mr. Hammond spoke did not suit his sense of importance. He continued his sentence, with dignity:

"For one, I am a good deal interested in the project. I like to meet people with brains, if I can boast of but few myself. Do you know, Mr. Hammond, whether any of the gentlemen of the Scientific Association are to be there?"

"Several of them have accepted invitations. I had a letter this evening from Professor John Whitney. He tells me that he has a hope of meeting me there. I have not seen him for five years and have had no certain prospect of ever meeting him again. It is a special delight to me to know that he is coming."

Will Gordon's eyes danced with delight.

"Professor John Whitney! He is the great naturalist, you know, St. John. He is an old friend of my father. Why, Mr. Hammond, will Father be invited?"

"He *has* been, and is looking forward to it with great interest."

"It is rather a mixed up affair, I should think — old and young, big and little, all together."

This was Larry Bates's comment. Larry wasn't certain whether he was in favor of it or not.

"That's the beauty of it," Lester St. John said eagerly. "A fellow doesn't always like to be mewed up in a corner with people of his own age. I like to meet people of mark."

"I don't know whether I want to go or

not," Larry Bates said, still good-naturedly. "I like to be where I am sure of having a good time, and the people are not too many miles above me. I don't believe they'll play croquet, and I like that better than science."

"But the music, Lawrence; what about that? However, there is no compulsion about it. Of course, you can go or *not* go, just as you please."

Miss Parkhurst came suddenly to the rescue.

"Why, of course you will go, Lawrence. I'm sure none of us will think of missing such an entertainment. For my part, I feel greatly honored by an invitation. Don't you think so, Mr. Hammond?"

"I certainly do. I know I never felt more honored in my life than when I received mine. I hope you will all avail yourselves of a very wonderful opportunity."

"He must be a wealthy man to be able to give parties on so large a scale," Fanny Horton said inquiringly.

"He is immensely wealthy and has resources at his command beyond any other person that I know. Well, what say you? Will you all accept the invitation?"

"Must we answer tonight?" was Sarah Blake's inquiry.

"Well, perhaps not necessarily. Still, of course it would be courteous to give a prompt answer. However, I'll not press you as to that. You can each return an answer for yourself."

"Because," continued Sarah, "the awful question of 'Wherewithal shall I be clothed?' might come in to bewilder some of us. It is a question that is forever haunting me, and I'm sure it will present its most formidable side for such a grand occasion as this."

This sentence, spoken in a kind of stage undertone, was sufficiently loud for Mr. Hammond to hear, and he answered it immediately:

"Ah, that brings me to a very important part of the subject which I had nearly forgotten. My friend has not only provided entertainment for his guests, but the 'Wherewithal shall I be clothed?' question is safely put to rest. He furnishes the wardrobe, also."

Such astonished exclamations as sounded among the eager group!

"I never heard of such a thing," said Fanny Horton.

"Why, Mr. Hammond, how can such a thing be managed?" May Horton exclaimed at the same moment.

"What on earth can be the object?" Celia Evans said, somewhat haughtily. "I'm sure, when I go to a party, I prefer to select my own wardrobe."

During this entire conversation Peter Armstrong had been gradually moving toward the circle, until he stood beside Mr. Hammond. Now he stood looking at him with wide-open, eager eyes. He had not spoken a word, but at this moment he answered the haughty Celia in sudden, solemn tones:

"You mustn't do that. You will be like the man who got in without having on the wedding garment; and they took him, and bound him, and cast him into outer darkness."

A sudden hush fell over the eager group, and Mr. Hammond repeated slowly:

" 'He that overcometh, the same shall be clothed in white raiment; and I will not blot out his name out of the book of life.' 'And white robes were given to every one of them.' "

Larry Bates broke in upon the hush with a little laugh and a quick sentence:

"Seems to me that's a kind of a sell, isn't it?"

Larry was never afraid to speak.

"In what respect?" Mr. Hammond

asked, turning toward him quickly.

"Why, I thought we were to go to some grand place and have a splendid time."

"I didn't promise that. I simply said you were invited. I cannot, of course, accept your invitation for you. Each of you will have to do it — 'each for himself,' in this as in many things."

Lester St. John was on the alert and spoke eagerly:

"But, Mr. Hammond, didn't you say a friend of yours was going to give an entertainment?"

"I did. How many times do you suppose the Bible illustrates the thought of heaven by telling of a feast, or a wedding, or an entertainment of some kind?"

"I'm *sure* I don't know, sir."

"Just look that subject up, won't you, and report to me some time?"

"But, Mr. Hammond," said Will Gordon, "didn't you *intend* us to think that you referred to some gathering not quite so far away, nor so bewildering in its route?"

"I intended to speak to you the exact truth about something that is certainly to come, and see to what extent I could enlist your sympathies and tastes. I thought you all seemed interested and animated. Does it lessen the interest because the gathering of which I speak, instead of being in some common home around you, is to take place in the eternal city, at the palace of the great King?"

"It's a different sort of thing from what any of us thought, anyhow."

This was Arthur Sanford's contribution to the conversation.

"Less important, Arthur?" his teacher asked quickly.

"Well, no — I suppose not, but not so easily managed."

"Some of us don't like the conditions," Larry Bates said, with a twinkle of mischief in his black eyes. "There are conditions attached to this party and, generally speaking, there aren't many connected with mundane ones."

"I shouldn't subscribe to that doctrine, Larry. Everything that is worth having in this world is based on conditions. But what is the fault in the ones of which you speak?"

St. John answered him quickly, and with a tinge of *hauteur* in his tones:

"The yielding up of one's will to the control of another — I object to *that*."

He spoke with the air of one who thought he had said a bold, defiant, almost impious thing, calculated to shock his listeners, and then waited to see how they would receive it.

Miss Parkhurst exclaimed in dismay, and even Celia Evans said:

"Why, Lester St. John, that's wicked."

But Mr. Hammond answered him with the utmost composure:

"I am surprised to hear you say so, St. John. I had given you the credit of being able to understand how superior intellects gloried in bowing themselves before powers infinitely superior to themselves."

St. John turned on his heel and moved away with a very annoyed face. If there was one thing above others that he coveted, it was being ranked among those who could appreciate superior intellects.

"Well," said Mr. Hammond, "all think of it, please. Some of you accepted the invitation. It *is* an invitation, more earnestly given than common ones ever are. The entertainment is certain to take place. If you are sincere in your acceptance, you will be there. I hope to meet you all. Can't we sing a verse together — something very familiar? Miss Nettie, can you play 'Sweet By and By'?"

It was a favorite hymn, and nearly all the voices united in singing it —

"There's a land that is fairer than day,
And by faith we can see it afar;
For the Father waits over the way,
To prepare us a dwelling place there.
In the sweet by and by,
We shall meet on that beautiful shore."

"That depends," said Mr. Hammond, "on whether we accept the invitation. Miss Parkhurst, can we have a word of prayer before I go? It is very pleasant to know that Christ is interested in even our amusements."

What *could* Miss Parkhurst do but bow her head in response to the question, though certainly it was the strangest conclusion to a dancing party that she had ever known. The prayer was very simple and brief, the two main thoughts being that their meeting together on the eve of an approaching Sabbath might not unfit them for the rest and joy of that holy day, and that the great feast that was being prepared above might not be forgotten by any one of them; and, that above all things, they might be kept from the misery of putting off their personal preparations until it was too late.

Immediately thereafter, Mr. Hammond bade them all a cordial good evening and took his departure. A general lull seemed to be upon the company. Just what to do next apparently bewildered them. Nettie Parkhurst still kept her station at the piano, with a grave face.

"Shall she finish the quadrille, or play the long meter doxology?" said Miss Celia Evans, inclining her head toward Nettie. "The poor child is evidently confused as to what is next in order, and no wonder."

"We've had enough of quadrille, I think," was St. John's verdict. "It *is* getting rather late for dancing."

Miss Parkhurst came to their relief by immediately announcing refreshments.

"Isn't he a queer man?" Miss Evans said to Lester, as they walked out to supper together.

"He is in earnest," Lester answered briefly.

"Oh, yes, he is in earnest. No one can doubt that; but don't you think he mixes things strangely sometimes?"

"What things, for instance?"

"Oh, well, like tonight. Wasn't it a strange sort of talk?"

"Perhaps so," Lester said, with a sarcastic laugh. "Yes, as things go in this world. I think it was so; but the question is, Which was the mixed thing for Saturday

evening at ten o'clock — what he introduced or what we did?"

"Why Lester! I'm half inclined to think
you are giving exclusive attention to this
sort of thing yourself."

"I'm a fool," Lester said moodily; "but I
may like to meet people who are *not*, for all
that."

"Ha, ha! Oh, ho! That is really the
richest thing I have heard this season." Mr.
Lewis removed his boots from the stove to
a chair in his glee, and then leaned back
and looked his friend over carefully before
he laughed again. "Ha, ha, ha! So you actually went to Miss Parkhurst's, on Saturday evening, too, and to meet your own
class! Why, man alive, don't you know that
Miss Parkhurst never has anything *but*
dancing parties and card parties?"

"She is a member of our church and a
teacher in our Sunday school," Mr. Hammond said significantly.

"Can't help that. She is an inveterate
dancer, too, as people without brains generally are, and she doesn't exercise
common sense in regard to time and
people any more than she does in regard to
anything else. I declare, that's too funny.
The idea of springing that trap on you!

That counts of your being so incommunicative as to your movements. I could have given you a bit of information. What in creation did you do?"

"What would you have done under like circumstances?"

"If you'll overlook the compliment, like circumstances wouldn't have found me under them. However, if I had been fairly caught, I presume I should have made the best of it — stood in a corner and chewed my whiskers during the performance, eaten my supper when the time came, and left at the earliest practicable hour, a sadder and wiser man. Now, what did you do?"

By dint of considerable cross questioning, Mr. Lewis drew out the story of Mr. Hammond's share in the Saturday evening party. His comment was, as he arose to go:

"Well, Hammond, there's no mistake about it — there are two kinds of people in this world, and two ways of doing things."

8

WORK THAT INVOLVES

MY "NEIGHBOR"

Mr. Hammond drew the shade, arranged the droplight to his satisfaction, and sat down at his green-covered round table to the uninterrupted enjoyment of his books. It was not often that he had an evening quite to himself. If there were not figures or ban books, or some of the bewilderments of business, there was a meeting of some sort — scarcely ever the luxury of an evening to dispose of as he chose. He appreciated it. He was an intellectual man, with tastes cultivated and education suited to the fond pleasures of a table on which lay several choice books and a review or two of the highest order.

This was the page of special interest that commanded his attention on this particular evening. Where his finger rested we quote: "And Jesus answered him, The first of all the commandments is, Hear, O Israel; The Lord our God is one Lord: and thou shalt love the Lord thy God with all thy heart, and with all thy soul, and with all thy mind, and with all thy strength: this is the first commandment. And the second is like, namely this, Thou shalt love thy neighbor as thyself. There is none other commandment greater than these."

It was with these last sentences that Mr. Hammond's reading suddenly stopped. The first part had served to solemnize his heart. He realized in a measure, at least, what an utter giving up of self, heart, soul, strength, mind, that word *all* involved. He realized how far short of the pattern his own copy of life measured. Yet he realized one other thing — and blessed is the man who, reading these words, can realize it — that he was trying to shape his life after that pattern. It was short, narrow, scrimped in every way, yet it was better than no garment at all, especially since, after all, it was only like the child's hemming that the loving mother endures because the child has done its best, and she can cover up the defects with some fine stitches of her own. No, not like that, either, because this earnest Christian man felt deeply that he had not even done as well as he could. There is, perhaps, no parallel to man's shortcomings and God's forgiving love. But it was over this sentence that Mr. Hammond halted: "Thou shalt love thy neighbor as thyself." His conscience had been busy all day, and, indeed, for several days, offering suggestions as to what he might do for a certain neighbor of his. It came to him now with quiet, questioning voice: "Whose ease and comfort and help are you working for now?" "But it is right," said Mr. Hammond's inner consciousness, answering this accusing voice. "It is right enough to take one's comfort occasionally. It is surely a proper thing to do to study my Sabbath-school lesson? Of course it is. 'Thy neighbor as thyself,' the command says. It doesn't require *more*. It is very rarely that I have a leisure evening."

"I know it. I don't know when you may have another opportunity to do that thing."

Mr. Hammond at this point pushed back his chair, put up his book, and took a measured walk up and down his room. His next inward sentence seemed somewhat irrelevant:

"It is raining quite hard."

"So it is, and so it was on Tuesday evening when you went to Professor Beyer's chemical entertainment. 'Thy neighbor as thyself' — nobody pleads for more."

"After all, I don't know that I can do any good."

"No, and you can't be sure until you try."

"But I might do harm."

"Was that remark yours or Satan's?"

Whereupon Mr. Hammond put an abrupt termination to this parley by coming over to the chair in which he had been sitting and kneeling down. It seemed quite time to consult higher wisdom than was to be found from any "inward consciousness." Apparently he found it, for he made no further talk; but, rising presently, put aside his books, got out rubbers and waterproof overcoat, turned down his gas to a very speck of brightness, and went out.

Miss Parkhurst was more nearly out of humor than circumstances often found her. The circumstances were sufficiently aggravating. In the first place, it rained hard. In the second place, she had a cold, had a strip of flannel about her throat, had an irritating cough that promised greater things in that line, unless it had a fair amount of attention. In the third place, there was an evening party just around the corner to which she had been invited. But how can one attend a party adorned with strips of flannel? Or how can one risk the exposure of its removal on a very rainy evening, especially with that cough thrown into the scales? Truth to tell, Miss Parkhurst would have found a way of reconciling or surmounting each of these difficulties if she had not possessed behind the scenes a somewhat sensible mother, at least so far as the body was concerned, who protested so strongly that she had to be heard. Therefore Miss Parkhurst rocked dolefully to and fro and sighed wearily and wished that it was eight o'clock, so that she might go to bed.

"You might go before eight," the mother said, trying to be sympathetic.

"It's stupid to go to bed," Miss Parkhurst answered, yawning; "but I don't know what else to do, and I really feel miserable. I don't believe I *could* hold my head up. There's the doorbell, Kate," as that official passed through the room to answer the summons, "if that should be anyone to see me (and it isn't likely it is — everybody worth seeing is at the party), you may bring them right in here. I'm not going into the parlor tonight for anybody."

The consequence of this direction was that Kate presently ushered Mr. Hammond into the cozy little sitting room.

"Why, Mr. Hammond!" Miss Parkhurst

said, and she held up her head without difficulty, surprise and unmistakable satisfaction in her voice. Then followed a very animated conversation, in which Miss Parkhurst's head and general health seemed to improve. The truth is, Mr. Hammond had the name of being exclusive. Certainly his calls in their set were rare, and upon Miss Parkhurst he had never called before. When you add to this the fact that most of the ladies had sense enough to both admire and respect him, it will in part account for her animation.

It was not until Mrs. Parkhurst had been summoned to a kitchen council by Kate that Mr. Hammond mentioned Sabbath school. Then he said, somewhat abruptly:

"I am interested in your class, Miss Parkhurst. Who of them are Christians?"

Miss Parkhurst looked embarrassed. She did not know. She thought, or she imagined — yes, indeed, she might say she was almost sure that Hattie Taylor was. For the rest, she didn't believe any of them ever thought of such a thing.

"You do not think, then, that there is any hopeful state of feeling — any special interest — among them?"

No, as far as she knew anything about it, there was not.

"Have you prepared your lesson for next Sabbath?"

"I haven't looked at it — don't even know what it is," she said lightly. "I have been sick all the week, you know. Besides," she added, as an afterthought, "I hardly ever look at it until Sunday morning."

At least she was not a hypocrite.

"Then perhaps you do not realize what a peculiarly important subject it is. I was struck with it this evening in reading. I felt the need of talking it over with some of my fellow teachers."

Miss Parkhurst felt honored.

"I'm sure I should enjoy it of all things," she said heartily, "though I don't know a bit about the lesson, and I'm a perfect dunce anyhow. What is the lesson?"

"Thou shalt love the Lord thy God with all thy heart, and with all thy soul, and with all thy mind, and with all thy strength." Mr. Hammond repeated the words impressively. "Isn't that tremendous, Miss Parkhurst? I tremble before that lesson. My boys are sharp enough to say, or at least to think, 'Physician, heal thyself.' How can I presume to teach such a lesson as that when I have hardly learned the alphabet of it myself?"

His counselor was utterly silent. He tried again:

"How are you going to teach it, Miss Parkhurst?"

"I don't know. I haven't the least idea." She did not say it carelessly or lightly, but as if she were in grave, thoughtful earnest. After a minute's silence she said, "I suppose I shall ask the questions on the question paper and have them read over the verses together, and let it go at that. That is about all the teaching that I ever do. I don't know how to teach, anyway."

"Neither do I," he said simply. "I feel my inability sometimes crushingly. Are you really well enough to talk about the lesson with me for a little while?"

"Oh, yes, indeed." She should like nothing better. Perhaps she should contrive to get some ideas, she said, and they were at all times scarce with her.

"Then," said this strange man, "shall we just have a word of prayer about it? You know what it says: 'If any man lack wisdom, let him ask of God.' I will pray, and then will you?"

Now I appeal to you, good, sensible reader; viewed in the light of common sense, could anything be more reasonable than that? Here were two people, members

113

of the same church, teachers in the same Sabbath school, having mutually confessed ignorance and desire for enlightenment. What was more natural than that they should bow down together before the God who has said: "If two of you shall agree on earth as touching any thing that they shall ask, it shall be done for them," and ask him for the help that he has promised? Yes, viewed in the light of actual Christian experience, could anything have been more utterly, surprisingly strange? Miss Parkhurst felt it so. She answered him, with cheeks aflame:

"Why, Mr. Hammond! I have never prayed before anybody in my life."

"No?" he said gently, "and you wouldn't like to make a first time of it tonight? Well, then, shall we kneel together and — 'the Lord looketh on the heart,' you know — I will offer the spoken words. But I trust we will be 'two agreed' as touching the 'one thing.' "

Do you imagine that Miss Parkhurst will ever forget that prayer? It startled — in some points actually frightened — her. It petitioned for a consecration of which she had never *dreamed*. It put a meaning into that word *all* that she had never imagined before. Some of the time she followed the language with a sort of vague longing that such a state of life might be hers — that she might some way jump into the experience which he seemed to possess, without any of the work of climbing; but more often she roved off into thoughts like these: "How queer this is. Here I am at a prayer meeting. I wonder what Belle Lawrence would say if she could see me now. I suppose they are dancing like tops over at the party. I hope Mother won't come in. What in the world would she think? He is a good man, anyhow — the best man in the world, I believe. I shall be more afraid of him than ever after this."

"Miss Parkhurst, why don't you attend the teachers' meetings?"

This was Mr. Hammond's first sentence after prayer. Miss Parkhurst hesitated. She had been asked that question before and had plead previous engagements, want of time, distance, dislike of going alone, and various other supposed to be courteous excuses; but immediately after such a prayer, simple truth seemed the only appropriate answer. So after a moment she said:

"Because I never have any time to study my lesson, and I am afraid they will ask me questions, and I am a dunce, you know."

"Do you really mean that you never have time to study?"

Again Miss Parkhurst hesitated. This time she laughed a little. Then she said:

"Well, no. I really suppose I *could* find a little time, if I remembered it."

"Won't you try it?" he said simply. "And if you will come to the teachers' meeting this week, I think you will find help. Have you any special engagement for Friday evening?"

Not unless her cold should prove one, she said, smiling. It had been very constant in its attentions for some time. By dint of much persuasion and a promise to call for her, she was prevailed upon to make an engagement for Friday evening.

"I don't know how they will handle it," Mr. Hammond said, referring to the lesson and the teachers' meeting. "It seems to me an immense topic for Christians — almost overwhelming."

"Why?" asked Miss Parkhurst, curiously. The idea of any Bible verses being overwhelming was a new and singular one to her.

"Why, the one verse is sufficient for a lifetime. 'With thy heart and soul and strength.' Did you ever think what that involved?"

She didn't know that she ever had, and she didn't understand it anyway. How could any one give *all* their love to God? It was certainly right to love people. And as for giving all one's strength, that had always seemed to her nonsense, so long as there were so many things that people had *got* to do. What does it mean, anyhow?

Mr. Hammond supposed it meant such a love for God as should make all other loves and interests subservient to this, and as to strength, all work in a sense was God's work, if it were manifestly one's duty to do it. Then one could do it for God, preparing to give an account, looking out for opportunities to serve him with it.

"Who works in that way?" Miss Parkhurst asked, with an incredulous smile.

"I don't know, but I think I know people who are trying to do it."

"Well, when they succeed, I should like to make their acquaintance, if I'm not too old by that time" — more incredulous still.

Did she really believe that such living was impossible? Mr. Hammond asked.

Why, yes, she did — very nearly so, at least. It was a practical sort of everyday world, and people had work to do that had nothing to do with serving God, so far as she could see. For instance, there was

Hattie Taylor, a good girl, she believed, if there ever was one, and poor as she could be. What use was it to preach to her about giving all her strength to God, when she had to work in the factory from six in the morning until six in the evening?

"I certainly know of no more important field for giving one's strength to God," Mr. Hammond said earnestly. "Her opportunities to speak for him, to act for him, to be faithful and consistent and patient for his sake are constant and never failing."

"Well, *I* don't know how to teach it," she said lightly; then added earnestly: "I'll tell you what it is, Mr. Hammond, I wish you had my class and I was one of the scholars. It is possible that even *I* might learn something by such an arrangement."

On the whole, the talk about the lesson did not amount to much. The lady was wandering in her attention and bewildering in her ability to slip away from the point under discussion, and yet she had gleams of earnestness. Mr. Hammond turned on the gas again in his own room at ten o'clock. The books looked inviting still, but he was a business man, working for others. He must not rob his employers of the clear, cool brain that only a full night of quiet sleep would give him. There was no time for study. He did not sigh, however, as he resolutely piled up the books and stacked them away on the shelves to await another evening of leisure. He did not even wonder dismally whether, after all, he had not wasted the evening. There is at least that amount of comfort to be gotten out of a disagreeable duty faithfully and conscientiously performed — the performer, by the time the work is done, has generally reached a higher place of life, where he can say: "I followed the path pointed out as nearly as I knew how. I did the work as well as I could. The results are not for me to arrange. The matter has been handed over to the Master's hands."

Some little review of the work is, of course, natural, and something of what Mr. Hammond thought of his must be gathered from his sole comment, made to the gaslight as he turned it out:

"At least she has promised to attend the teachers' meeting. Perhaps she may find enlightenment there."

9

BLIND WORK

There was another occupant of the parlor at Miss Parkhurst's on Friday evening when Mr. Hammond was shown in — a gentleman lounging on the sofa with a very much-at-home air. Mr. Hammond restrained a look of surprise and bowed somewhat distantly.

"Good evening," the gentleman said, with an air of great composure. "Pleasant evening. Have a seat here, Hammond?"

"Thank you," said Mr. Hammond, taking a chair instead of the proffered sofa.

"You and I are intent upon the same errand, I presume?"

"Indeed!" Mr. Hammond said, with uplifting eyebrows and an unmistakable accent of surprise. It was a most unusual thing for him and that gentleman to be intent on the same object.

"You are waiting to see Cora, I take it?"

"Miss Parkhurst has an engagement with me for the evening."

Mr. Hammond's tones were more dignified than seemed at all necessary.

"Is that so?" his companion said, in some surprise. "That is certainly bad for my plans."

Mr. Hammond took a book and absorbed himself in the title page. Mr. Tracy seemed suddenly to have a new idea and scribbled on the back of a calling card which he took from the card case. If Mr. Hammond had been looking over his shoulder, he could have read this:

"What in the world does Parson Hammond want of you? I want you to go with me to see the Royal Marionettes. They are unique. Don't disappoint me and hurry down if you have any compassion. Hammond and I don't assimilate."

Then he strolled to the door and summoned little Mary, who was frolicking in the hall, and gave her a wee handful of raisins to pay for carrying his note up to "Cora."

"How provoking!" Miss Parkhurst said, pausing in the hurried making up of her toilet to read his card. "George always *does* come for me when I can't possibly go. I wonder what possessed me to promise to go to teachers' meeting? I don't know how to tell George — he won't like it — and Mr. Hammond won't like it if I *don't* go.

How provoking men are!" and she dropped the note and rushed hurriedly through the process of donning skirt and overskirt and basque and necktie and pin and cuffs and sash. You ladies all know about how long that took her. I suppose it will occur to your critical minds, just here, that she could and ought to have been dressed before. Let me explain. Her afternoon dress was fashionably long, and she had dragged it through several streets making calls; hence its unsuitable condition for the evening, discovered at a late hour, and all the bewilderments of a second toilet had to be gone through with. The evening's complications were growing more bewildering. While she nervously drove a pin without any point into her finger instead of her ruffle, the doorbell rang again, and a third person, unknown to either of the others, awaited her coming in the parlor. All three of the gentlemen arose as she made her hurried entrance soon after.

"Mr. Hammond," she said, smiling brightly as she shook hands, "I am real sorry to have kept you waiting, but I am tardy by nature — never in time anywhere. George, I have an engagement for this evening at a teachers' meeting."

"Teachers' meeting!" echoed the said George, in wide-eyed wonder. "Teachers of *what*, in creation?"

"Why, Sabbath-school teachers, you ignorant fellow. Didn't you know they had meetings every week to study their lessons?"

"I am sure I didn't. Can't they get along without you this evening? It is a special occasion, you know. The Royal Marionettes are not always in town, and teachers' meetings, it seems, *are*."

"Have you seen these performers, Mr. Tracy?"

Mr. Hammond asked this question, his great gray eyes fixed searchingly on Mr. Tracy's face.

"I have had that amusement. Have you? Rich, isn't it?"

"Remarkably," Mr. Hammond said, dryly.

Then the strange gentleman:

"Pardon the interruption, but my errand is pressing. Miss Parkhurst, I believe. I bring a message to you from one of your scholars," and he produced a crumpled bit of paper.

The bewildered look on Miss Parkhurst's face deepened into dismay as she read.

"Sarah Blake is sick, and she wants *me*."

She volunteered this information in a startled, exclamatory tone, with a marked emphasis on the *me*. The gentlemen received it variously.

"Of course, then, I relinquish my claim on your time," Mr. Hammond said promptly.

"So do *not* I," Mr. Tracy said gaily. "Who on earth is Sarah Blake, and what possible claim can she have on *you?*"

"She is one of my Sunday-school girls."

Then Miss Parkhurst turned away from him and spoke, with dismay still in her voice:

"Mr. Hammond, how can I possibly go? I shouldn't know what to do or say!"

"What is the matter with her?" interposed Mr. Tracy.

"I'm sure I don't know. This note is from the mother, and so queerly spelled that there isn't much to be made out of it. Do *you* know anything about them, sir?"

The strange gentleman bowed.

"I am the attending physician. The daughter, Miss Sarah, is very ill indeed — fever of a noninfectious type. It became my painful duty this evening to tell her that I feared she could not live, and she almost immediately begged that you might be sent for. She was so importunate that I feared to have her refused, and as I was coming in this direction, I volunteered to bring the message. I trust you will pardon my saying that even this delay is dangerous to my patient."

"Under the circumstances, of course, you will go at once. You cannot do less. I shall be glad to show the way there and render you any assistance in my power."

Mr. Hammond's voice was prompt and earnest.

"I don't see the thing in that light at all," Mr. Tracy said hotly. "Sunday-school teachers don't engage to run into all sorts of dangerous places, incurring the danger of contagion —"

"I assure you there is nothing of *that* sort," interposed the physician.

"And undergoing unnecessary fatigue and exposure," continued Mr. Tracy, paying no sort of attention to the doctor's remark.

Miss Parkhurst, in her turn, utterly ignored him. He was eminently a man to be ignored when people were in earnest.

"But, Mr. Hammond," she said, and the distress in her face and voice was genuine, "what could *I* do? I don't know anything about sickness. I never had anything to do with it, and I'm afraid to go where anyone is dying. *Is* she really going to die?"

This last to the physician.

"I'm afraid there is very little hope, if any."

"Then, I beg of you, do not lose any more precious time. You surely would not refuse a request from one dying? She may have a special petition to make of you, and you can surely point her to Jesus."

Thus petitioned, Miss Parkhurst turned hurriedly to Mr. Tracy:

"George, I really think I will have to go. I'm sure I don't know a thing to say, but I suppose I ought to go and see her anyway. It won't make any difference with you, for I positively had an engagement with Mr. Hammond. So you must both excuse me."

Meantime Mr. Tracy had a new idea. He spoke in a low tone:

"Perhaps I might go down with you, and you speak to the girl, and then after that we might look in on the Marionettes. They are really comical, Cora. I want you to see them. Could we manage it in that way?"

"I'm sure I don't know," she said nervously. "I don't know what I'm going to do or say, only I suppose I ought to go and see her, and I know I don't want to. Well, I'll go right away and have it over with."

Then the four went out into the street and their various ways. The strange doctor bowed and went on uptown to see a patient.

Mr. Hammond said, in low tones, "I will call in the course of an hour," and went to teachers' meeting.

"Does Parson Hammond expect to find *you* there in the course of an hour?" Mr. Tracy said, as he drew Miss Parkhurst's hand through his arm.

A frightened, bewildered household they were at Mr. Blake's. They were a large family, accustomed to high health and boisterous, rollicking ways. They were poor; not miserably so, but as poor as a good, industrious foreman in a shoe factory, with house rent to pay and seven young mouths at home to feed, to say nothing of the seven pair of feet to be shod, is likely to be. Sarah was the oldest child. You remember her, the sharp, keen one in Miss Parkhurst's class — the one who always had a quick answer ready for any possible question? The fever had burnt out all her sharpness. She lay like a ghost among the pillows — wan, large-eyed, and helpless, a mere shadow of life. Only this evening had the doctor, in answer to her searching questions, revealed the probable

127

truth that she was dying. She was too weak to be frantic — almost too weak to be frightened.

The house was full of people passing in and out, good, kindly, willing neighbors; but among them all, Sarah could not recall one who would be likely to tell her how to die. She thought over her acquaintances, the girls at the mill. There was Hatty Taylor, but she had gone in the upper mills, five miles away. Not another one would know anything about it. The scholars in her class — she almost curled her weak, parched lips at thought of them. *They* couldn't tell. The minister — yes, but Sarah Blake, with all her sharpness, had always been unaccountably and painfully shy of the minister. She was afraid of him now. Miss Parkhurst — and here she hesitated, as no Sabbath scholar ought to be obliged to hesitate over her teacher. She had doubted all her life whether or not Miss Parkhurst knew anything about religion. "But perhaps she does," she murmured wearily to herself, shutting her hot eyes for a moment, trying to close out the intolerable light. "At any rate, she is the only one *I* knew. She is a member of the church. That Mr. Hammond would come, I guess; but, then, I didn't accept the invitation.

Besides, I don't want to see him. I'll send for Miss Parkhurst. I must have someone. I shall go wild if I don't."

Into this house, with its frightened and noisily crying occupants, came Miss Parkhurst, as frightened herself and as much disposed to cry as the veriest child among them. She went in alone to the sickroom, Mr. Tracy reiterating, as he left her at the door, that he would call in twenty minutes and take her to see the Royal Marionettes.

"How do you do?" she said, standing at the foot of the bed and speaking in a hollow, unnatural voice. "I'm sorry you are sick."

She had never seen the ravages of fever before on a familiar face. It seemed to her that this must be Sarah's spirit.

"I have sent for you," said Sarah, speaking slowly and with great solemnity, "because I want you to tell me how to die. You ought to know. You teach in Sunday school, and you ought to be able to teach that. So tell me what to do."

Miss Parkhurst shivered visibly, but she tried to speak in a more natural tone:

"Oh, Sarah, don't talk so. You are going to get well, I hope, and have real good times."

Sarah made a movement of impatience.

"Can't you tell me anything?" she said, almost sharply. "What do you pretend to teach for, if you can't?"

"She don't rightly know what she is saying," Mrs. Blake said, taking her apron from her eyes and speaking apologetically. "The poor thing, she has been kind of flighty all day."

Sarah turned her great, hollow eyes on her mother and spoke deliberately:

"Mother, I know just exactly what I'm saying. The doctor says I am going to die, and this lady professes to have learned how to die, and I want her to teach me. Now, can you do it?"

"Why, Sarah," Miss Parkhurst said, trying to speak soothingly, "you must trust in Christ, you know."

"How shall I do it?"

"Why, just trust in him to take care of you and don't be afraid."

"Is that all there is to religion? And, even if it is, how am I going to help being afraid?"

"Why, he'll help you, you know."

"I don't know anything about it. Why *don't* he, then?"

"Why he *will*, if you love him."

"But I don't love. I'm afraid of him, and I'm afraid to die. Aren't you? If you lie here in my place, wouldn't you be in the least afraid?"

Miss Parkhurst trembled so that she shook the foot of the bed on which she leaned, but she answered truthfully:

"Yes, I should be afraid, but it is because I haven't lived right. There is no need to be. All people are not. Grandfather wasn't."

"That doesn't comfort me much. I haven't lived right, either, and now the living is all done, and here I lie. What next?"

She spoke more quietly but with intense earnestness.

"Sarah, you must pray," her teacher said, with equal earnestness.

"I don't know *how* to pray. That is one of the things that I never learned. *You* pray for me. Kneel down here, now, and let me hear *you*. Perhaps it will give me courage."

Over in a chair by the window sat Mr. Blake, the shoemaker, his head bowed in his hands, but every nerve keenly alive to what was going on. *He* didn't know how to pray. At the head of the bed stood the weeping, prayerless mother. Half a dozen children were gathered around her, all sobbing. The nearest neighbor, who acted as nurse, stood in the doorway leading into the sitting room, indulging every now and then in that dreadful sickroom whisper, with a neighbor who had come to inquire. Both of these eyed her curiously. She had come from a different world than theirs. She felt certain that neither of them knew how to pray. Yet this Christian lady of education, of culture, felt that she could no more kneel down in the presence of this company and pray for that passing soul than she could lift the roof and escape through it from this dreadful place.

"I'll read to you," she said, with trembling haste, and looked about her eagerly. The Bible was a proper book to read on such occasions, and she nervously seized upon Sarah's own Testament, lying covered with dust among the few books on the shelf. Opening it at random and turning the leaves with great and increasing embarrassment (being not too familiar with the sacred pages even in her calmest moments), she presently began to read, in the utmost doubt and confusion. This is what she read:

"And when they were come to the place, which is called Calvary, there they crucified him, and the malefactors, one on the right hand, and the other on the left. Then said Jesus, Father, forgive them; for they know not what they do. And they parted his raiment, and cast lots. And the people stood beholding. And the rulers also with them derided him, saying, He saved others; let him save himself, if he be Christ, the chosen of God. And the soldiers also mocked him, coming to him, and offering him vinegar, and saying, If thou be the king of the Jews, save thyself. And a superscription also was written over him, in letters of Greek, and Latin, and Hebrew, THIS IS THE KING OF THE JEWS. And one of the malefactors which were hanged railed on him, saying, If thou be Christ, save thyself and us."

At this point the reading was interrupted by a muttered sentence from Sarah:

"Miserable wretches, the whole of them, to ridicule a dying man! I wonder he didn't strike them dead."

Miss Parkhurst read on rapidly:

"But the other answering, rebuked him, saying, Dost not thou fear God, seeing thou art in the same condemnation? And we indeed justly; for we receive the due reward of our deeds: but this man hath done nothing amiss. And he said unto Jesus, Lord, remember me when thou comest into thy kingdom. And Jesus said unto him, Verily I say unto thee, Today shalt thou be with me in paradise."

On and on she read, no sound breaking the story until Mrs. Blake touched her arm and whispered:

"You needn't read any more. She has gone off into one of them heavy sleeps. She does so a good deal."

And the nurse added more information, in a sepulchral voice, at the other elbow:

"The doctor thinks she'll go off in one of them sleeps. I shouldn't wonder if the time had come."

Miss Parkhurst drew her breath in heavily. The strain upon her to read even those Bible verses had been tremendous. She had not taken in their meaning in the least. She had chosen them without knowledge or direction; therefore they were not intended to help her, and they didn't. She even didn't know what she had been reading; yet it is doubtful if the wisest could have made a better selection. Did you notice how into those few verses was crowded the very length and breadth of human cruelty, and the very height and depth of divine forgiveness?

Miss Parkhurst looked about her doubtfully.

"I might go home, now, I suppose?" she said inquiringly.

The mother looked dismayed.

"If she *should* wake and want you," she said pitifully, "I don't know what we would do. It isn't the *doing*, you know, Miss Parkhurst. You could sit here in this rocking chair and not do a thing. There's people enough ready and willing to work, only there ain't one of them belongs to the religious kind. If you *could* stay awhile, Miss Parkhurst, I'd never forget it."

There was a little bustle out in the sitting room, and presently Miss Parkhurst was summoned thither. Mr. Tracy was waiting to see her. He spoke eagerly:

"Come, Cora, hurry! It is late, but I have reserved seats, and we'll get considerable of the fun. People are going in crowds. The Marionettes take better here than I thought they would. You look wretchedly flushed. I suppose the air of that room is horrid. How is the girl? Be as expeditious as possible, because it really is quite late."

10

NERVOUS WORK

"I am not going, George," she said, as soon as he gave her opportunity. "Sarah is very sick, and they seem to want me. I can't do any earthly good, but I can really do no less than stay awhile."

Mr. Tracy made an impatient movement.

"I think that is *nonsense,* Cora. As you say, what good can you possibly do? Infinite injury to yourself, as likely as not. I don't like it at all, and I'm sure your mother would disapprove. You really *ought* to excuse yourself and come with me."

To her own surprise, Miss Parkhurst, who was usually ready to be led wherever the person in company with her chose to lead her, found herself feeling little or no inclination to go in search of the "Royal Marionettes." She had lost the desire to hurry away from that sickroom; a sort of fascination seemed to be about it. A little sense of disappointment lingered in her mind because of her engagement with Mr.

Hammond. She had not known that she cared particularly for the teachers' meeting until then; but about those Royal Marionettes, over whom Mr. Tracy was enthusiastic, she had come to care very little. She hated to be urged, because it was so much her nature to do what she was coaxed to do; the quality of resistance had been so long unused that the power to use it was nearly lost.

"But I *can't* go, George, don't you see," she said, half impatiently; it seemed tiresome to him to urge her. "It really wouldn't be decent; they expect me to stay awhile. They take it for granted that I am going to do so, and there is no chance of getting away."

"I wouldn't be imposed upon in that manner," Mr. Tracy said loftily. "This sort of people generally have friends of their own class. It isn't likely they are so entirely dependent upon you. If you could do any earthly good, why the case would be different; but, by your own confession, you are quite useless. You are too easily led, Cora."

Voices and steps in the hall, and Mr. Hammond appeared in the little room. Miss Parkhurst turned toward him eagerly:

"I'm real glad you have come. I wish you had been here half an hour ago, you might have been of some use. I'm sure *I* wasn't. She was awake and conscious, but I am afraid she won't be again."

"I excused myself at a very early hour from teachers' meeting in order to hear from her," Mr. Hammond said, by way of explaining his present appearance. "How does she seem?"

"She seems very sick, and she looks dreadful. I should hardly have known her. Mr. Hammond, do you see any use of my staying? They want me to, but I can't do anything."

"Of course there is no use in it," Mr. Tracy broke in, eagerly. "It is folly for them to expect it merely because the girl happens to be in her Sabbath-school class. Miss Parkhurst isn't used to scenes of this kind; she ought to be away."

"The house of mourning is a very difficult place to go from, Mr. Tracy, provided people are really desirous of your presence." Mr. Hammond spoke in his coldest, most dignified manner, and Mr. Tracy answered irritably:

"Such people are always pushing themselves into notice."

Miss Parkhurst was shocked.

"Why George," she said earnestly, "the poor girl is dying."

"Well," he said, impatiently, "even if that should prove to be the case, you can't keep her alive by your presence, I presume."

Then there came a fourth person into the scene, the doctor, with that unceremoniousness which belongs to doctors in houses where they are looked for and expected, pushed open the door and entered without invitation.

"How do you find her?" Mr. Hammond questioned.

"Very low, and yet the pulse is firmer than I had expected it would be by this time. You may give the preparation in the tumbler once in two hours and moisten her lips quite frequently; that is about all that can be done for her. I think now that she will linger through the night. Are you to have the care of her during the night?" This last sentence was asked suddenly, as by one who had just thought of the possibility of something different.

Now it would be difficult to imagine a human being dropped into this working world who had hitherto led a more butterfly existence than Miss Parkhurst. She absolutely did *nothing*, and did it industriously, too, from Monday morning until Saturday night; the one oasis in this desert of idleness being her Sabbath-school class, and you remember how she taught that. By this statement I do not mean that she sat down and folded her hands; on the contrary, she was full of engagements, and generally in a hurry. I simply mean that she *did* nothing.

Imagine, if you can, how such a one would feel brought into the atmosphere of everyday work of the forlorn and unpoetical sort and looked to for help and comfort! A night watcher! She had never been that in her life, not even in the third-rate sense of the term, where all one has to do is to look after a fire that needs very little looking after and wait for reports from the next room, where the *real* watchers are at work. Miss Parkhurst had been up until midnight, oh, yes, and until two, and, on rare occasions, three o'clock; but nothing more heavily freighted with responsibility than a party or a sleigh ride had occupied her mind, and here she was in a two- or, at best, a three-roomed house with a dying girl, separated from her only by a board partition and an earnest-faced doctor looking down at her and saying, "There seems to be no other responsible person." Was she *actually* a responsible person?

The doctor waited courteously, Mr.

Hammond looked on curiously, and Mr. Tracy walked the floor in a fume, while Miss Parkhurst tried to settle the question with herself. It did not take her long. Two natures, perhaps I might say three, were struggling for the ascendancy. She shrank from it all; death was full of a nameless terror to her; she had never seen anyone die, she did not *want* to see anyone, did not want to die herself, nor think about it; that dreadful time was to be put as far away as possible; the odor and the quiet and the sorrow of a sick and poverty-stricken room were all alike intolerable to her — this was the ascendant nature: but there came to her a sudden sense of importance, an accession of dignity. She had never before stood face to face with a person who seemed to expect her to assume responsibility, as this doctor evidently did; he thought she could do what up to this moment she had not imagined possible. She glanced over at Mr. Hammond: He stood aside, as one who had no business to interfere in the matter, yet the wonderment as to how it would end was apparent in his face. "He thinks I won't do it," said Miss Parkhurst to herself. "I suppose he thinks I can't, and the doctor thinks I *can*." Then there was the third nature, the element of pity. She was sorry for them all, those forlorn people out in the other room, and that sick girl. In much less time than it has taken me to write this, Miss Parkhurst turned to Mr. Tracy.

"George, could you call and tell Mother what has become of me? She will be anxious, for she has had no message."

Mr. Tracy was dignified. He replied haughtily that he would "do her bidding, of course"; then he went away without bestowing even a bow upon Mr. Hammond.

At last they went away, and the house settled down into a midnight quiet. Miss Parkhurst, in a dress entirely unsuited to the place and the work, unfastened ribbons and chain and belt and made herself as comfortable as she could under the circumstances, then sat herself down to await with what patience she could the coming of morning. I don't suppose that those who have never tried it have the least idea how long the morning *can* tarry. Nothing to do, nothing to read, bound in honor not to go to sleep, not particularly given at any time to the enjoyment of solitary thought, what *was* there to occupy such a mind? Truth to tell, however, Miss Parkhurst had not the least desire for sleep; on the contrary, her eyes seemed to herself to be fastened open with weights that would never again run down and give her a chance to rest.

Probably Miss Parkhurst will never in all her life forget that night of watching. The clock struck three after the lapse of what seemed a century of waiting. She started and looked about her nervously. The lamp, turned low, cast long shadows across the uncarpeted floor. The sick girl lay absolutely motionless upon the bed. The watcher bent over her. Was she sleeping or was she dead? What if she should die before morning, and she be left alone with a corpse? She who always avoided even *looking* at a corpse when she went to a funeral. "What possessed me to stay?" she said in a tremor of fright. "If Mr. Hammond were only here, he might take care of his protégée himself. I will never be caught in this way again, I am sure of that."

She grew calmer after having assured herself that her patient was still breathing, but it was a strange feeling to realize herself the only one awake at that weird hour. Then she remembered that other sleepless Watcher, that All-seeing Eye, looking ever down on her, and so far from quieting her, it very nearly threw her into another spasm of fear. She wasn't used to such companionship.

Mr. Hammond, on his way downtown, met his friend Mr. Lewis, and to him he gave an account of the evening's experience.

"The man is utterly repulsive to me," he said, in an annoyed tone. "I hate to meet him in any place where I feel obliged to hold conversation with him, because I feel that it is a waste of time, and I don't want to have anything to do with him."

"What sent you in search of Miss Parkhurst in the first place? Not exactly companionship, I suppose?"

"Oh, didn't I tell you how that was? Well, the starting point was rather peculiar perhaps. I settled myself one evening last week for a quiet time over the lesson. You know I seldom enjoy the luxury of sitting down alone to work on anything but daybook and ledger, and I was really rejoicing over the prospect; but the lesson proved to be that commandment which reaches into one's very heart, 'Thou shalt love they neighbor as thyself'. It came home to me very forcibly what a striking illustration of its neglect I was. There I had made everything comfortable for myself without as much as remembering that I had a 'neighbor.' I concluded it to be my duty to look up a neighbor and try to do something for him. Something that I overheard from Miss Parkhurst's class — you know her class is in close proximity to mine — decided me to see if I couldn't give her an impetus in the matter of preparing her lesson; so I called on her, and out of that grew the invitation to the teachers' meeting."

Mr. Lewis walked beside his friend for a few steps in silence, then he said suddenly:

"But see here, Hammond, Tracy lives two blocks nearer you than Miss Parkhurst does."

Mr. Hammond looked at him with a puzzled air.

"What are you coming at?" he said at last. "I don't understand you."

"Oh, nothing — only I am somewhat bewildered as to the geography of my 'neighbor,' and I thought I would try to find enlightenment."

"I don't know but I am extremely obtuse, but I really don't get your meaning," and Mr. Hammond looked more bewildered than before.

"Why, you seem to object to Tracy's company and haven't the least idea of trying to do anything for his advancement, and I naturally wondered at just what geographical distance the 'neighbor' idea came in."

Light began to dawn on Mr. Hammond's mind — rather, it burst upon him suddenly.

"I see the point," he said, stopping in his walk and looking earnestly at his friend. "You are right, Lewis, I have entirely ignored the idea of 'the great commandment,' except where it pleased my taste to obey it. I'm much obliged to you. Things never appeared to me in just this light before."

"You are in such horrid earnest about everything," Mr. Lewis said with an amused laugh. "I wonder what other individual of my acquaintance would give a second thought to a hint like that; but you will go and practice on it like a martyr. I know you will, and I shall be responsible for any amount of boredom that Tracy chooses to inflict on you. I wish I had kept still."

Mr. Hammond answered only the first part of this sentence.

"You must be very unfortunate in your choice of friends," he said, smiling, "if you honor me as the only one of the number who would conscientiously follow out a new thought after it had been presented to them."

"I only judge them by myself," Mr. Lewis said, with an expressive shrug of his shoulders. "I can see things now and then as plain as anyone; but to follow up my eyesight is quite another matter."

At the corner the two men separated, and each went home with a new idea. In the gray light of the early morning, Miss Parkhurst went homeward. A lonely walk it was; she had not realized that the streets were ever so deserted and silent; she had never been on Arch Street before when there was other than a whirl of people and wagons and business; now she found herself starting nervously at the sound of a solitary footstep behind her and experiencing a feeling of unutterable relief at the discovery that it was only a milkman hurrying after his milk wagon. Placards on every side of her announced in flaming letters "The Royal Marionettes." How queer the letters looked to her, and how absurd the dancing puppets seemed. She hadn't the least idea that she should ever want to see the creatures. They reminded her of Mr. Tracy, and she was surprised and a little shocked to discover that there was a sore feeling of disappointment in regard to his words and actions of the evening before. There were reasons why it wasn't pleasant to Miss Parkhurst to feel other than satisfied with Mr. Tracy's acts. At the door of her own home, her mother met her with a troubled face and anxious words.

"My dear child, how could you think it to be your duty to do so wild a thing as to sit up all night? George was in *such* a state of mind over it! I never saw him so excited, and I don't wonder. I really think Mr. Hammond took a great deal on himself, and might better have been attending to his own affairs."

Either loss of sleep or her own thoughts had made Miss Parkhurst nervous.

"What in the world do you mean?" she said testily. "Why *shouldn't* I sit up as well as anyone else? And what do you suppose Mr. Hammond had to do with it? Somebody had to sit up, you know."

"But it was such a strange idea for *you.* Why, I don't think you ever did such a thing in your life before. They must be queer people to expect it."

"There has to be a first time, you know, Mother," Miss Parkhurst said, speaking more quietly than before. "I am in perfect health, and there is no sort of reason why I shouldn't do my share of the disagreeable things that there are to do in this world. I don't suppose anyone really enjoys sitting up."

This was such an entirely new sentiment coming from Miss Parkhurst's lips that her mother was surprised into silence, and the daughter made her way upstairs. She looked about her room with a bewildered air; it was strewn with articles that she had displaced in her hurry of the evening before, and they called to mind her plans and feelings. Was it possible that she thought and felt, and did thus and so, only twelve hours before? It seemed at least a week ago. She felt older and graver; in fact, Miss Parkhurst felt womanly. She had been in a responsible place and borne her share of the burdens and the anxieties of life for the first time, and it had already done its work on her heart. Mrs. Parkhurst came up presently, bringing a cup of tea.

"You better drink this," she said, "and then try to sleep. I'm afraid you will be sick. How is the girl, anyway? Is she living? George said you thought she might not live till morning, and I was dreadfully worried about your being in such a place."

For some reason this sentence also grated on her daughter's ears.

"She is living," she said gravely, "but she is very low. I don't suppose she can live long. But, Mother, why shouldn't *I* have been there as well as anyone? We have all got to die, I suppose."

This sentiment, so different from any that she had ever heard from her daughter, sent Mrs. Parkhurst downstairs silent and wondering. Something had happened to her that her mother did not understand.

11

LEARNING HOW TO WORK

She went to teachers' meeting at last, though it was three weeks after her first invitation to do so. There was a very uncomfortable feeling of embarrassment about going, it seemed so strange, to have been a Sabbath-school teacher for three years, in a church where weekly teachers' meetings were held, and never attend one, then suddenly present herself; also, she had a wholesome horror of being asked questions. I find myself constantly meeting with sufferers afflicted with the same disease. I wonder if it is universal in its influence?

"Miss Kitty," I say to a bright little teacher in our school, "won't you come to teachers' meeting this evening? We are very anxious to have a large attendance."

Miss Kitty fixes a pair of bright blue eyes on my face and answers promptly enough, "I'll come if Professor Wheeler will promise not to ask me any questions."

Fancy a teachers' meeting in which no questions are asked! Now it so happens that Miss Kitty is a fine scholar — one of the best in our normal school — and Professor Wheeler is one of the favorite teachers in that same school.

"Kitty," I said, "what if you should try to make an agreement tomorrow, that Professor Wheeler should not ask you any questions in geometry?"

"Oh!" Kitty said, flushing and laughing, "that is another matter. Of course I must answer questions in class."

Now, why is that such an entirely different matter? To be sure, Miss Kitty spends a good deal of time in the preparation of her school lessons; but surely a Christian teacher in a Sabbath school would not go before her class without careful preparation of the Bible lesson that she is expected to teach them! I confess that the whole subject is full of mystery to me.

"I'm almost sorry I came," Miss Parkhurst said, with an embarrassed little laugh, as they neared the parsonage. "I'm two-thirds afraid of Mr. Gordon at any time; and if he looks at me tonight, he will frighten me out of my wits."

"I didn't know that you were such an exceedingly timid lady."

Mr. Hammond was unable to keep a

little touch of annoyance from sounding in his voice, and deep in his heart he was thinking, "How is it possible for a grown-up young lady to be so silly!"

Miss Parkhurst laughed again. "Oh, well, I'm not particularly timid, under ordinary circumstances," she said brightly. "But a minister, you know, always frightens wicked people like me, especially at his own house, where he has one at a disadvantage. I don't know what to do with the lesson next Sunday, anyway: I wish we could skip over it. I'm glad, though, that they're in the Old Testament once more."

"Do you think Old Testament lessons easier to teach than the New?" Mr. Hammond said, surprised, and a little pleased. His opinion was the same, but he had not looked for sympathy from her.

"Yes, I do; ever so much," she said heartily. "At least, we find something fresh, something that we don't know anything about. The very names are hard enough to puzzle us, but the lessons, this long time, have been about things that we have known all our lives. All the children learn verses in the Gospels, you know, and say them over and over; I did it myself; I learned the first chapter of John, for instance, and said it as a new lesson to every teacher I had, for several years; and I averaged a new teacher a month, I think?"

"Your Sabbath-school experience was unfortunate," Mr. Hammond said dryly. He had retired to the depths of disgust and annoyance again; Miss Parkhurst's reasons for liking the Old Testament as a textbook better than the New were different from his. "There is one consolation," he told himself, as they ascended the parsonage steps, "she certainly needs the help of the teachers' meeting; I am glad I went for her. But what a burlesque hers is on Bible teaching!"

The parsonage study was full; comfortably so; and a very pleasant looking group they were; they made room at once for Mr. Hammond, and if they were astonished at his companion, they had the grace not to say so.

Miss Parkhurst, on her part, was a little astonished; it didn't look like a meeting. "They all look as though they had come out for a good time," she said to herself. Just why a company of Sabbath-school teachers, met to talk over the lesson, shouldn't have a good time doing it, Miss Parkhurst didn't stop to explain to herself.

"Hammond, you are losing your good name; you are late," Mr. Lewis said, as he made room for his friend beside him. "This is the second time in a month, too."

"Never mind me," Mr. Hammond said, smiling. "What about the lesson?"

"We haven't made great progress," Mr. Gordon said. "We are still lingering over the first verse; there is a division of opinion as to the most striking thought. Mr. Lewis is our secretary, and he sits, pencil poised in air, waiting to bring something tangible out of the confusion of ideas. Take up the verse, please; we want your opinion."

"There is so much," Mr. Hammond said promptly, with the air of a man who had been thinking about this very verse, "I don't know what to choose from the many thoughts."

Miss Parkhurst looked at him with a curious, half-incredulous air; to her, that first verse of the lesson was a bare statement, nothing more.

Mr. Hammond read the verse: "And Joshua said unto Achan, My son, give, I pray thee, glory to the Lord God of Israel, and make confession unto him, and tell me now what thou hast done; hide it not from me."

"The first thought that impresses me," he said, "is the tenderness of Joshua's address, 'My son.' I can seem to see the brave old man, brought to grief by the ill-doing of one of his followers, yet with his heart moved with a deep pity for him."

Then they launched into full tide of talk over that first bare verse, and Mr. Lewis used his pencil industriously, and Miss Parkhurst grew more and more amazed; she had not known of that way of studying lessons.

"Now," Mr. Gordon said, at the close of a busy hour, "we come to the important question: What are we each going to do with this lesson for our classes?"

Miss Parkhurst had not the least idea what he meant.

"My class are children, you know," Mrs. Ames said. "I have thought to make my important point, 'The progressive nature of sin,' as explained by poor Achan himself. First, you know, he looked, then he wanted, then he took."

"I have very much the same idea," Miss Willard said. "I have been making little paper ladders for my class. I have named the ladder, 'Covetousness.' The sides are composed of Achan's helpers; his eyes, heart, and hands; then the different work that each of these helpers did for him compose the rounds."

"You might give him a guideboard, made

out of the golden text, 'Beware of covet-ousness.' " This item Mr. Lewis added.

"Sure enough, so I might!" she said, with enthusiasm. "I mean to do it."

Miss Willard was the infant-class teacher and had a large class.

"Fifty little ladders!" Miss Parkhurst thought to herself. "Oh dear! What an immense amount of work, and what a queer idea! I wonder how she happened to think of it?"

"My point is," said another, "how near Achan was to the Land of Promise, and what a pitiful thing pulled him down into the depths: a piece of gold and a few pieces of silver!"

"And the handsome garment," Miss Hall said; "don't forget that. I'm going to call the attention of my girls to the fact that the love of pretty clothes was a snare, even in the days of Achan."

"One of the saddest features of the entire lesson is, I think, the suffering that Achan brought on his friends. They had to suffer with him, even as they do now, for the sins of others." This was Mr. Hammond's contribution to the general fund.

"What about the personality of the lesson?" Mr. Gordon asked. "Do we have any people led away nowadays by this same sin of covetousness?"

"Plenty of them," Mr. Lewis said, scribbling away very fast.

"Can't we have some illustrations on that point from some of you?"

Several were ready with suggestions.

"My Allie has been coveting your Robert's pony all day," Mrs. Ames said, in a half-laughing undertone to Mr. Smith.

"There is a good deal of coveting of pretty jewels, and pretty homes, and pretty clothes, in these days," said Miss Hall.

"Miss Hall can't forget the goodly Babylonian garment," Mr. Lewis said, laughing.

"Well, I *can't*. I think the sin is committed more often in that way than any other; at least among the young people?"

Miss Parkhurst listened in amazement. How freely they talked together about these things! They spoke of Achan as if he had been a man in their midst, instead of a faraway myth, as all those Bible characters had seemed to her. Mr. Gordon had hitherto refrained from asking her any direct question. He suddenly turned toward her: "Miss Parkhurst, you have not given us the principal point, as it has struck your mind tonight — have you a crumb for us?"

Mr. Hammond, having been previously warned, looked for nothing further than a refusal; he could only hope that it would not be a silly one. As she had come to the meeting in his company, he felt in some degree connected with her, and he bent his head over the Bible, with a somewhat heightened color.

Miss Parkhurst's voice was low and grave. "Yes," she said, "I have made one point plain to myself tonight; that is, my utter unfitness for a Sabbath-school teacher."

There was a moment of awkward silence; others besides Mr. Hammond were astonished at this answer. Mr. Gordon called first. "Then you have made a very important point," he said earnestly. "Without having such a realizing sense of this as will lead us to keep very near to the great Teacher, there is no true teaching."

Very soon after that the secretary was called on for his report. "Mr. Lewis," his pastor said, "have you succeeded in unraveling this tangle of ideas that we have given you and setting them down in logical array?"

Mr. Lewis laughed. "I have done my best," he said cheerily, "but you have been a hard set to keep track of tonight." Then he began to read slowly, and with frequent pauses, a synopsis of the different thoughts that had been called out during the evening; at the same time the teachers fell to work with pencils and notebooks, and Miss Parkhurst, looking over Miss Hall's shoulder, discovered that they were engaged in taking an abstract of what Mr. Lewis was reading.

"There," said Mr. Gordon, as he folded his paper, "we have a commentary on the lesson that will suit us better than any of the printed ones, because it is original."

12

WORK TO BE DREADED

"I don't know how to teach in that way," Miss Parkhurst said, as she took Mr. Hammond's arm for their homeward walk.

"In what way?" he asked. Not that he did not understand her, but he was undecided how to answer her remark, and it seemed as good a way as any in which to gain time.

"Why, the way that you all talked tonight. I don't know how to fit the lesson to present times and present people. The only thing I can do is just to ask questions about what happened in those times and let it go at that. I want to give up my class, anyway. I think that is the best thing to do; I have thought so ever since —" and then she stopped.

"Ever since when?" he asked her, speaking gently. He was very anxious to learn whether this feeling of fitness had any depth, or was only a passing fancy.

"Ever since that night I sat up with Sarah," she said, speaking slowly and with evident effort. "Thought about a good many things that night. It was the longest night I ever had, and among other things was this, that I wasn't just the one to teach girls like Sarah; such girls, you know, as have to depend on their teacher for all their religious knowledge; it frightened me, and I said then that I wouldn't do it anymore; but I have had a habit of going to Sunday school for so long, that I hardly knew how to give it up; but tonight I made up my mind that teaching isn't my forte. I don't know how to do it, you see."

"Has it never occurred to you that there was another way out of the difficulty; that you might reform your manner of teaching, if you are not satisfied with it?"

Mr. Hammond spoke very kindly and encouragingly. He was surprised that his companion had such a depth of feeling about this matter. He had not given her credit for it.

"No," she said, speaking in her old light tone. "I never thought that preaching was my vocation; and the sort of teaching that you and the rest of them recommend is no more nor less than preaching; I never could do it in the world."

"Preaching is simply teaching, of course," he said coldly. "If our clergymen felt that they were doing no teaching of any

162

sort, they might be justified in feeling discouraged." His manner had become dignified again; the truth is, this gentleman was very anxious that people should be perfect and felt impatient with those who fell far below his ideal. His words had the effect of making Miss Parkhurst more indifferent than before.

"I can't help it," she said gaily. "I am not fitted for a preaching teacher, or a teaching preacher, whichever you choose to put it; I *know* I am not; and the best thing I can do is to resign."

If she expected an answer to this, she was disappointed. Mr. Hammond had no answer ready. Truth to tell, his honest opinion was that unless she could do better work than by her own confession she had been doing, the resignation would be the best thing; but he was not quite prepared to tell her that, so he kept silent.

In no very amiable mood, Miss Parkhurst parted from him at her own gate and went in to meet Mr. Tracy, who lounged on the sofa in his usual careless attitude and waited her coming.

"What an age you have been!" was his greeting. "I'm inclined to think that I shall begin to complain of that Parson Hammond before a great while."

163

The lady's amiability was not proof against this sentence. She answered it very coldly. "I suppose you would hardly recommend his leaving me to come home alone, would you? I have been to teachers' meeting."

Mr. Tracy threw his head back among the sofa cushions and indulged in a low, not unmusical, laugh. "That is really the funniest part of the funny performance," he said, when his laugh was over. "It is impossible for me to conceive of you as a Sunday-school teacher anyway; and the idea of you sitting up there in the parson's study with these starched-up fossils is too ludicrous."

What *was* the matter with Miss Parkhurst? Every word that he spoke jarred on her nerves. She answered in the same cold tone: "I don't know what you mean, I am sure; why shouldn't I teach in Sabbath school as well as any one of them?" How astonished her conscience must have been, to hear her rush over to that side of the question, after laboring to convince Mr. Hammond that such was not her mission!

Mr. Tracy laughed again. "Why, my dear," he said indolently, "you don't seem like them, that is all, and I'm very thankful that you don't. Let us dismiss the subject. I have invitations for the hop, tomorrow evening, and I want you to be ready by eight, for our set are going to have a little private entertainment before the general fun begins."

"What hop?" said Miss Parkhurst, and there was not only surprise but consternation in her voice.

"Why, don't you know about it? Oh, no, I had forgotten that I didn't see you last evening. By the way, where were you? Did Hammond have you at a prayer meeting? Why, Dick, you know, has opened his new parlors, or, rather, he means to open, after tomorrow; and before that time he gives a little entertainment to his friends — an oyster supper, with a little dancing."

"But, Mr. Tracy, you know I don't attend hops, least of all at hotels."

Mr. Tracy laughed again. "Did I call it a hop?" he said, good-humoredly. "I was thinking of the grand opening which is to take place next week; this is a very informal affair, as you may imagine by the informality of the invitation; in fact, it is nothing more than you have at your own house."

"Only, our house is not a public hotel." She spoke as if she thought this ought to make a difference.

"Nonsense!" he said gaily. "Neither is this — is not to be until after tomorrow; why, there are not more than forty invited, and those are our intimate friends."

"I do not think I shall go." Miss Parkhurst said, this in a low, half-dejected voice.

Mr. Tracy raised himself to an upright posture and looked at her steadily: "Cora," he said, half-anxiously, "what is the matter? Do you know that you don't appear in the least like yourself? You haven't appeared so for a long time; I am really concerned about you. Can't you tell me what is the trouble?"

I am not prepared to say that Cora did the most sensible thing that could be done, or gave a reasonable answer to the question, I am only stating facts. What she did was to sink down on the sofa, on the opposite corner to that occupied by Mr. Tracy, put her head in one of the unoccupied cushions, and begin to sob. It was not very loud, nor very wild crying, but a low, tremulous sobbing.

Mr. Tracy was utterly horrified. During his long acquaintance with this lady, he had never seen her other than bright and cheery — a cheeriness almost amounting to giddiness. He had never fancied that she could cry. He bent toward her, with a confused idea of comforting her, and not an idea as to how to do it. She shrank away from him with a petulant gesture. She was not at all in the mood to receive comfort from him. Her movement vexed him, and he sat back in the corner and frowned. Then he went to casting about in his mind for a reason for this strange change. "Ever since," he said to himself, "why, let me see, yes, ever since that evening that I came for her to see the Royal Marionettes, she has been unlike herself. That *Hammond* was waiting for her then, and I declare she has been under his influence more or less ever since; it is just his tombstone manner and conversation that have given her the blues." At this point he began to think aloud:

"That troublesome fellow! I wish he would keep away from you. It is just his influence that has changed you in this way. I could choke him and keep a serene countenance during the operation."

Then it was that Miss Parkhurst rose into dignity; she was not a particularly dignified young lady; indeed, I doubt if anyone had ever thought of applying that adjective to her; but there was that in her companion's words which aroused swift indignation in her, and she spoke accordingly:

"George, I can't imagine any excuse you can have for such language as that; I infer that you are speaking of Mr. Hammond, as you have several times hinted something of the same sort; however unjust and foolish such insinuations may be to him, they are certainly almost insulting to me, and I beg that you will do me the kindness to spare me the hearing of them in the future."

Her cheeks were glowing, and her eyes had so unusual flash in them. What her friend, who might be supposed to feel rebuked, thought at this juncture was, that she really looked exceedingly pretty, prettier than usual, and a spice of indignation was not at all unbecoming. He laughed good-naturedly, congratulated himself inwardly that at least he had succeeded in checking her tears, which was the important point, and said:

"Come, Cora, don't let us quarrel; we never do, you know; we have always been models in that respect. It is growing late, or at least I have but little time to spare. You used up so much of it at that teachers' meeting. What do you find to talk about that takes a whole evening? I presume they have a royal gossip. Well, let us settle about tomorrow evening. You can be ready by eight, can you not?"

Miss Parkhurst was not ready with her reply. In her mind was this sentence: "I will call for you tomorrow evening a few minutes before eight. You will be ready by that time, will you not?"

The remark had been made, not to her, but she had overheard it. Two of the teachers were talking, and she knew the subject of their words was the teachers' prayer meeting, held every Saturday evening. She had never been in her life.

"Don't you know that tomorrow will be Saturday?" she said, turning suddenly toward Mr. Tracy, a curious wonder in her mind as to whether he would understand what she meant.

"Why, yes," he said, speaking slowly and looking as she imagined he would, rather puzzled. "I know, of course, that it will be Saturday — what then? Oh, I suppose I see the point; you are afraid of trenching on Sunday. No, you need have no fear of that, in fact, that is the reason why we meet so early, to allow for a good social time before midnight. I'll engage to promise you that you shall be safe inside your own gate by that hour." In his heart he muttered, "That is some of that poky Hammond's work, I'll venture. She wasn't so particular last winter."

"The teachers' prayer meeting is tomorrow evening at eight." She didn't say these words to him. It was simply thinking ahead. In her mind was a feeling of the contrast between the ways that different teachers had of spending Saturday evening, but Mr. Tracy felt called upon to answer.

"Indeed!" and there was more than slight annoyance in his tones. "What an important affair this Sunday-school teaching is! I don't think I ever before realized the magnitude of the business. Do they impress all the evenings of the week into their service? It is fortunate for me that they don't enforce their laws, isn't it! Is it possible that the clock is striking eleven? I promised to look in at the clubroom at ten; as you see, the sin of that omission will have to be laid at your door. But, Cora, I really must go and give you a chance to rest. I want you to look your brightest tomorrow."

Hereupon Miss Parkhurst found voice to say, "George, I am sorry, but I don't think I can go tomorrow."

"Not go! Why, I am sadly disappointed. I counted on a pleasant evening with you.

Aren't you feeling well?"

"No!" she said, abruptly, "or, yes. I suppose I am well enough to go, but I am not in the mood, and you know I never *did* do things unless I felt like doing them. I am not one of the sort who could go to a party or anything else from a sense of duty. I go or stay, simply because I want or don't want to; and as it happens to be, I *don't* want to this time; you will have to take the consequences."

Mr. Tracy smiled incredulously. "You are tired tonight," he said good-naturedly, "and I think you have very little idea of what you do or do not want. I will just look in, in the morning, on my way downtown and get a more favorable answer to my petition; and remember that I shall be very much disappointed if you do not accompany me. I have reason to think that you sometimes do things to please me."

Then he bade her good-night, and she went to her room in a very unenviable state of mind. I think one of the worse features of her trouble was that she hadn't the least idea what was the matter with her, nor where to seek for a remedy. She knew that the hitherto unbroken brightness and merriness of her butterfly life had been rudely broken in upon, and that she was uncomfortable and unhappy; she vaguely traced the beginning of her unrest to that night spent in watching; and had been saying to herself for some weeks that her nerves had been shaken by the unusual scenes, together with the night watching, and that the disturbance of heart and life arose from this; but it did not seem in the least reasonable that a watch of one night should so disturb the current of her life; that after weeks of calm she should not get back her usual cheerfulness, and the shadow, instead of lifting, grew worse; it was not that she was never her old self, but these frequent and horrible seasons of gloom were growing upon her; she began to be seriously annoyed; she enjoyed being happy; she could not endure the thought of discomfort in any form; certainly not that which touched herself; yet here she was, in the very depths of it; there were some things that she knew about it; for instance, she knew that it had its outgrowth in fear. During that night of watching she had discovered that she was afraid of death, absolutely horribly afraid; that the very thought of another messenger coming to her filled her with miserable dread and terror; that the terror deepened, rather than vanished.

Just where all this commotion of thought

would end it was impossible to tell; something more than thinking is required in order that persons may be really benefited. So far as any actual help was concerned, up to this date, she might as well not have thought at all; indeed, thinking was a thing that she hated to do. If she could have glided back to the surface period of her life, when her thoughts, if she had any, were not defined enough to be troublesome, she would have been content. But here was this vexatious question of the hop to be thought about! She sat herself down in great bitterness of spirit to discover, if possible, what she really *did* think, and just why she had been moved to decline Mr. Tracy's invitation.

13

WORKING FOR A MIRACLE

Those who came in contact with Miss Park-hurst the morning after the teachers' meeting had no reason to think that it had improved her. She was unaccountably irritable. The truth was, her mind was occupied with the question of the Saturday evening hop. She dreaded Mr. Tracy's influence over her; she had too long been in the habit of doing as he said not to feel inclined to do it now. At the same time, she was honest in not wanting to go to the hop; just why she didn't desire to go, she did not understand; she only knew that the place and the people whom she would be likely to meet were all at variance with her present mood; then, too, the associations from which she had so recently come were so utterly at variance with her usual surroundings that she recognized, as she had not before, the inconsistencies between her life and its professions. The question was still unsettled when she went to breakfast; and she sipped her coffee and pronounced it "too sweet," and then "too weak," and then not hot enough, all the while having a miserable sort of feeling that she was being ill used in being made to think and decide.

"There is a note from Miss Kelly, saying that she cannot do another thing until you come and see about it; and unless you come this morning, she is afraid she cannot be ready by tomorrow." This information her mother gave, as she passed the repaired coffee for the third time. "I opened the note last night. It came while you were away, and I thought there might be something to attend to at once."

Miss Parkhurst's face brightened. Miss Kelly was the dressmaker. She certainly ought to see about the work as soon as possible, for she really needed her dress for tomorrow. It was after eight; Mr. Tracy generally went downtown about nine; it would never do to wait until after his call; Miss Kelly had, of course, been at work since seven o'clock. It wasn't fair to keep her waiting any longer. She would go at once; then she should put off the annoying discussion until one o'clock, at least, for he could not leave the bank before that time. How fortunate it was that Miss Kelly should be wanting her on that particular morning! She finished her coffee in haste, and only came back when she was halfway down the steps, with her message:

"Mother, George said he would run in on an errand on his way downtown, but I cannot wait for him; tell him that I was obliged to go out in haste, and that if he wants to see me, he must try again." And then she was off.

As she walked briskly down Chestnut Street, a new idea came to her. What if the decision should be taken out of her hands in this way — a sort of miraculous intervention? She certainly didn't want to go to that party; it didn't seem just the way to spend Saturday evening anyway; she would be very glad of an excuse to keep her from going; there used to be plenty of miracles in old times about smaller things than these; she didn't see why there shouldn't be such things nowadays; in fact, there *were;* she had heard Mr. Gordon say he had been *kept* from doing thus and so. What did he mean, if not something like this? It was a most blissful discovery; it would save her from thinking anything more about the troublesome matter; she would just give herself up to the press of circumstances. If the Lord hedged up her way, so that she could not go to the party, why, of course it would be absurd in George to be offended with her.

Very much exhilarated by this state of things, and believing herself quite as worthy of having miracles performed for her as ever Joshua was, she met Miss Kelly with a bright face. It surprised even Miss Parkhurst, who was on the lookout for miracles, to see what a number of errands there were to do that morning that seemed to demand immediate attention. She was genuinely astonished when, on reference to her watch, it appeared that it was ten minutes after one o'clock, and Miss Kelly raised her window and called to her as she passed the door: "I must really detain you a moment, Miss Parkhurst. We have found it impossible to match the shade of velvet in the city and we want to consult with you as to what is to be done."

The lady in question ran gleefully up the steps, thinking as she did so, "The bank opens again at two. Wouldn't it be strange if I should be detained so as to miss his afternoon call? I should really feel as though I had been led to just this arrangement." There was something ludicrous in this being led to spend an afternoon in search of a particular shade of purple velvet in order to be kept from the disagreeableness of coming to a decision, but the ludicrous side did not occur to Miss Parkhurst; and she dallied over her decisions in a way that was quite a trial to Miss Kelly's patience.

It was ten minutes to two when she left the house, charged with a commission to order some cambric from Beldon & Moshier's, to be sent up immediately. The firm of Beldon & Moshier was away downtown. At any other time, Miss Parkhurst would have left too tired to have taken the errand; but she was engaged in helping out a miraculous intervention of Providence this morning, and, of course, was bound to do her best. She walked home from the store in a very complacent frame of mind, congratulating herself that it had occurred to her to take Crawford Street instead of the shorter and pleasanter route that would have led her past the Iron Bank; for a *tête-à-tête* with Mr. Tracy was, of course, to be avoided.

"Poor George!" she said, as she ran up the steps of her mother's house. "I wonder if he will be vexed? It does seem too bad; I suppose he went out of his way to call this noon, but it really wasn't any planning of mine. I don't see how I could have helped it; now there remains the planning what to say to him this evening, or perhaps he will get discouraged and not try it again. I do believe I will go to the prayer meeting to-night. I am a teacher, and I really ought to be there; it won't make much difference, though, if I give up my class. I wonder if I shall give it up?" Then she went in and sought her mother in the dining room, eager for an account of Mr. Tracy's state of mind. "Has George been here?" she said, the moment she caught sight of her mother, ready to sit down to the waiting lunch table.

Mrs. Parkhurst shook her head. "I haven't seen him," she said. "That greasy little Tommy, who does the bank errands, brought a note here about ten o'clock. I should think they might find a more respectable boy to work for them. What a time you have been! I could have a wedding outfit planned in this time. I thought I should faint. Where have you been all the while?"

"Where is the note?" said Miss Parkhurst, and at that moment, spying it beside her plate, she seized it. There were barely three lines:

DEAR CORA:

A press of work has detained me from calling. After all, it will make no difference, though; with the brightness of the morning, I am sure that your brightness must have returned. Be ready at eight promptly, if possible, as it is quite a drive.

As ever and in haste,
GEORGE

What an ignominious end for a miraculous undertaking! Instead of wearying herself, in her trip through the city, so far as her affairs were concerned, she might as well have sat quietly at home. She went upstairs in an irritable and ill-used state of mind. The miserable decision was no nearer its making than before.

"Well," she said, in an injured tone, "I don't see but I am to be compelled to go, in spite of my attempts to avoid it; I'm sure I can't be blamed; I have struggled hard against it." And then her mood changed, and there came a feeling very like complacence over her, in the thought that she had struggled against circumstances, using Providence as a helper, and circumstances had been too much for them both. She by no means put it in this irreverent way. She would have been utterly shocked had anyone suggested to her that such was her state of mind; but when people go to attributing their own foolish evasions of decisions, in that imbecile way, how else can you put it?

You will not, I think, be surprised to hear that half past seven found our lady hurrying through the mysteries of her toilet, in eager haste to be ready for Mr. Tracy at eight o'clock. She had decided that it would not do to let that gentleman come for her at that late hour, fully expecting her company to a place where fashion decreed that gentlemen should be accompanied by ladies, and then disappoint him. I think myself that it would be a very shabby way to treat a gentleman; but Miss Parkhurst had ignored the fact that there was such a thing as writing a note; that would have involved a decision on her part, and we have seen that she had determined on leaving the entire matter in the hands of what she chose to call "Providence."

Her schoolgirl sister came up the stairs two steps at a time and tapped at the door.

"The two antagonistic forces of your being are downstairs," she said, leaning over a chair and watching the effect of a blue bow in her sister's hair. "What am I to say to each of them?"

"What?"

"Why, the two elements that are contending for your approval, or your company, or something, are waiting below, each eager for a message; George represents the world, the flesh, and the other one, perhaps; and Mr. Hammond is solemn enough just now to stand for the other side, whatever they call them. I am not so familiar with their synonyms."

"Mr. Hammond! Is *he* there?"

"He is. The two gentlemen arrived almost together. At least, I had just seated Mr. Hammond when George came."

Miss Parkhurst looked annoyed. This was an interposition that she had neither planned nor expected.

"I won't see him. I shall have to go with George now, anyway."

This she said talking to herself. But she said it aloud, whereupon her wise young sister laughed.

"Tell Mr. Hammond that I have an engagement this evening and shall have to be excused, and tell George I shall be ready in a few minutes."

This was her message, and yet at that moment, in her heart, she had a Pilate-ish sort of feeling that she had washed her hand of the whole matter and was being led whither she would not.

The two gentlemen in the parlor below had each an uncomfortable feeling, as was usual when they came in contact; Mr. Hammond's call had been actuated by a feeling of self-reproach, in part, and in part by the hope that the most indifferent teacher that he knew in the Sunday school was on the way to improvement. He had seen hopeful signs during part of the previous evening but had finally parted from her in such an annoyed state of mind that he felt as if he never wanted to see her again. During the day he had reproved himself for his hasty and faithless spirit, hence his call this evening. It was just possible that he might persuade her to go to the teachers' prayer meeting from whence he hoped that she might gain an impetus to be found nowhere else.

No sooner was he seated than Mr. Tracy made his appearance. He, on his part, was excessively annoyed on seeing the occupant of the sofa. He had been in a troubled state of mind all day and was by no means sure of his lady's company for the evening. As his note indicated, he had reason to know that she could be obstinate when she chose; she might choose now, and there were reasons why it would be especially trying on this particular evening. His face grew dark with frowns as he recognized Mr. Hammond, and he inwardly vowed that if Cora had made an appointment with him, he would give her an opportunity to choose which of them she would keep for a friend.

Mr. Hammond, remembering his friend Lewis's caution in regard to the gentleman before him, roused himself to be courteous.

"Have you an engagement with Miss Parkhurst this evening, may I ask?" he said courteously, as the two gentlemen waited the return of their messenger. "I ask that I may know what my probable success will be. I called to invite her to our teachers' prayer meeting, not knowing but she may have other plans."

Mr. Tracy's spirits rose. This fellow was not ahead of him then. He might as well have a little fun.

"I believe I have," he said, with great positiveness. "If I mistake not, we are to enjoy the private hop that is given at the new hotel this evening. We ought to be on the way by this time, but ladies are never quite ready for an engagement, at least so far as promptness is concerned." And then he gave himself up to the enjoyment of the evident disapproval, not to say horror, on the face of his listener. He knew enough about the ways of "the cique" — which word he was fond of applying to those Christians whose lives were stamped with their belief as plainly as this man's was — to understand that a Saturday evening *hop* would not be deemed the most desirable place in the world for a Sabbath-school teacher.

Mr. Hammond was spared the necessity of a reply by the arrival of Miss Parkhurst's regrets; and he went away, feeling that it was no sort of use to try to do anything for her, and he should drop all effort in that direction, and that he would advise a change of teachers for that class of hers the very first opportunity that he had, and all the while, I suppose there had never been a time in her life when she more needed help than she did at this moment. For when a Christian woman adopts the silly notion that to float with the tide, without an effort to judge understandingly and prayerfully as to the right and wrong of question, is "being led by Providence," she is in a dangerous state of mind.

14

UNWELCOME WORK

It was such a lovely Sunday morning! The world looked just as glad and happy as a world can look. The church bells seemed like joyful music; that is, they sounded so to some people. What a pity that people and things can not be in tune in this world. Now I am obliged to confess that these same church bells sounded like jangling discord to Miss Parkhurst. They made her head ache; they made her hair snarl, or something did. She twitched a hair pin out nervously, flung it on the floor with an impatient exclamation, and drew a long sigh.

"It isn't conducive to health to go to a hop on Saturday evening."

This her young sister said, in a tone of mock sympathy, bestowing a mischievous glance at the lady before the glass, from under a veil of hair that she was parting in the middle.

"I wish you wouldn't persist in calling it a hop." Miss Parkhurst spoke in irritable voice. "Can't a small company of friends meet each other for an hour in the evening without having the children talking about hops?"

The "child" laughed merrily.

"An hour! Oh, Cora, you know the clock struck twelve long before you came in. I should think a church member ought to have conscientious scruples against dancing parties on Saturday. Milly Burns says she has gotten over her prejudices against that class of people. She used to think that she would never join a church in the world, but she would just as soon be a member now as not. They are not a bit different from other people."

"Milly Burns is a silly girl, and you are another. If you talk nonsense all the morning, you will be late to Sabbath school, as you usually are."

With which sisterly caution Miss Parkhurst finished tying the bow to her sash and swept haughtily from the room. This was unusual talk between the sisters. The younger one was given to sarcasm and sharp-sightedness, but her good-natured roommate was in the habit of meeting all her words with merry laughter and playful answers.

Miss Parkhurst did not wait for her sister to complete her toilet. She was in no mood for waiting this morning. She had come to a decision at last: This was to be her last day in the Sabbath school; she was not fitted to be a teacher, she said, in a miserable fit of humility. The girls should have someone who could do better for them than she ever had. She took credit to herself for speaking so plainly about this matter.

"It is not shirking," she said, with a dismal sort of complacency. "I am perfectly willing to continue this work, only I see plainly that I am not fit for it. Some people are suited to be teachers, and some are not. I am clearly one of the latter. George has seen this plainly enough this long time. I dare say others have seen it and talked about it. I shall give them up. I haven't the least idea that I ever did them any good. I don't know how to do it. But I shall miss them, I know I shall. I don't believe I shall know what to do with myself for a few Sundays. I have been in school so long, it will seem queer not to be hurrying to get there before the opening exercises are over."

This was Miss Parkhurst's soliloquy as she walked slowly down the shady side of the street toward the Harvard Street Church. She was early. There had been that in her decision, or else it was in the strong coffee that she drank late at night, which had prevented her morning nap, and for almost the first time since she could remember, she was in her place among the very early ones, earlier than the superintendent, for which she was sorry. She wanted to talk with him and have the matter over. She was nervous and unhappy. The decision hadn't given her heart the rest and relief that she had hoped from it.

"He is a great superintendent," she told herself, in an irritable aside. "He might know that the teachers would like to consult him."

And yet this was the first time that she could remember of being present to see whether he was there or not. He was unaccustomedly detained. Teachers and scholars filed in, but no superintendent. Her own class filled, and the girls exchanged glances of surprise that she knew were called forth by her early appearance. Every one of them knew where and how she had spent Saturday evening.

Mr. Hammond came and took his seat at her left with a grave bow. He was surprised, too. She wondered vaguely just when their paths would cross again and realized that in severing her connection with the Sabbath school, she was cutting herself off from association with people like him.

"He won't call on me anymore," she said, and a little flush gathered on her face. "But I don't care; George will be more comfortable anyway, and I suppose I shall be, too. I've been pulled two ways long enough. I'm sure I'm tired of it."

At the very last moment the superintendent bustled in, with the air of a man who was late and knew it. There was no time to appeal to him then, though Miss Parkhurst had fully meant to decline teaching the class that morning. Her thoughts were suddenly turned into a new channel by the arrival of Sarah Blake, just as the opening hymn was being announced. Contrary to the expectation of everyone, that young lady had recovered. More than that, the night that her teacher had spent with her was the one on which the favorable change had taken place. It was five weeks since that time, and Miss Parkhurst, though hearing from her occasionally, had not been near her since, and it was with a feeling somewhat like that which one might have on seeing one come in whom they thought dead that she looked upon her. She had never realized that Sarah was to get well. The girls greeted the newcomer with a show of kindness and interest. She moved in different spheres from most of them; but she was human, and so were they; and they realized for a moment that she had come back to them from the edge of the grave. As for Miss Parkhurst, this but increased her embarrassment. She had learned just enough about the lesson to realize that she did not know how to teach it. With the memory of those solemn sunken eyes as they had last looked into hers, she felt that she *could* not teach it.

During the singing and prayer, she decided as to her course of action. She meant to say to them, "Girls, I am going to give up the class. I don't know how to teach you. You ought to have a better teacher than I have been, and I mean you shall!" She took great credit to herself for her determination to speak thus plainly about herself. Then she thought they would talk the matter over about getting such a teacher as they would like, and what with the library books and their usual difficulty about being suited, they would contrive to get through the half hour without any attempt at that awful lesson, which was so bristling with personal questions, according to the views that the teachers in their

Friday evening meeting had taken.

No sooner was Mr. Gordon's voice hushed than she turned toward them, with the prepared sentence on her tongue. But Sarah Blake was ahead of her, speaking eagerly:

"Miss Parkhurst, I have wanted to see you and the girls so much. I wish you could have come to see me, but after the dreadful night I gave you, I was afraid to try again. But I knew you would be so glad of what I have to tell you. Miss Parkhurst, it is all so different; it is just as you said and as you read. I shall never be afraid again. I have found out how to die and how to live. Oh, Miss Parkhurst, I shall never know how to thank you!"

There was surprise and bewilderment and consternation on Miss Parkhurst's face, all struggling for the mastery. Surprise, to hear Sarah Blake talking in this unknown tongue. Why, Sarah Blake had been almost, if not quite, a scoffer. Bewilderment, that anyone could speak thus freely and familiarly to her on this embarrassing subject, and actually announce her as a helper. Consternation, because in this new and strange development she did not know what to do or what to answer. There was another feeling struggling to gain notice, and that was a strange little thrill of pleasure. Had she really helped someone? And on this, of all other subjects! It was very strange. And — why yes, it was pleasant. But what was she to say? Sarah gave her little chance to reply.

"Now, Miss Parkhurst, I want to go to work. I have wasted all my life, so far, and when I found out this wonderful thing, and then thought I was going straight to heaven, just as the man you read me about did, why, it had its sorry side even then. I wanted to do one little thing to show how glad and how happy I was, and I said to myself, if I should get well after all, oh, how I will work, and now I mean to! And you must show me how. What can I do? It has been so hard to wait until I got well enough to come here. I wanted to talk with you so much. Tell me what I can do."

This was certainly the English language, and yet it sounded almost as unfamiliar to Miss Parkhurst's ears as if it were an unknown tongue. How did she know what was to be done, or how to do it? Yet with what new, strange respect did this girl wait for her answer, seemingly assured that she was the very one to help. It certainly was pleasant, even though it was the most embarrassing question she had ever been asked in her life. Meantime, Sarah waited.

"I don't know," her teacher said, slowly, timidly. "There are things to do, of course, but just how or what," with long pauses between the words. "They have prayer meetings, you know."

Sarah caught at the words.

"Girls' prayer meeting, do you mean, Miss Parkhurst? So they do, and I would like that. You would, too, wouldn't you, Mary? And, Miss Parkhurst, you would lead them, wouldn't you? Let's have one this very week."

"Oh, my patience, no!" Miss Parkhurst said, frightened out of her bewilderment. "I never could do such a thing."

Sarah smiled incredulously.

"Oh, but, Miss Parkhurst, you know I remember what you did for me! Mr. Newton," she said, catching at the superintendent's sleeve as he passed, "we want a prayer meeting; will you appoint it? For the girls, you know, and Miss Parkhurst to lead it. Not any of the other teachers, because we shall be afraid of them. When would be a good evening, girls? Don't you think Saturday would, because we get out from the factory earlier?"

Mr. Newton looked scarcely less bewildered than Miss Parkhurst. He wasn't quite certain which surprised him most, such a proposition from Sarah Blake's lips, or the announcement of Miss Parkhurst as leader. He half suspected that a rude joke was about to be attempted. Something of this fear showed in his face, for Sarah hastened to say:

"We mean it, honestly we do, Mr. Newton. Miss Parkhurst suggested it herself."

"It is an excellent idea," he said cordially, and turning with new interest toward Miss Parkhurst. "What evening do you decide? I shall be only too glad to announce it. Where are you to meet?"

"Sure enough," Sarah said. "I really hadn't thought of that. If we could meet with you, Miss Parkhurst, or would it be too much trouble?"

Thus questioned, with Mr. Newton looking on and listening, with Celia Evans laughing and enjoying it all as a new sensation, what could poor, puzzled Miss Parkhurst do? She was being led, whither she would not. Some faint memory of her recent frantic search after a miracle came to her, and with it a hurried question as to whether this was not a miracle that had come without her seeking or desire. And then she said hurriedly:

195

"Why, you can meet in our parlor, of course."

How absurd it would be to refuse. And Mr. Newton went back to his desk with a pleased smile on his face.

"It gives me great pleasure and encouragement to make one announcement," he said, a little later. "On Saturday evening of this week there will be a young ladies' prayer meeting at the house of Miss Parkhurst, No. 346 Lafayette Place. There is a general request that the young ladies of our Sunday school will respond to this invitation. I am glad to tell you that this suggestion comes from one of our teachers, who is deeply interested in its success."

Now, of course Mr. Newton may be pardoned for thinking that every word of this was true. But imagine, if you can, with what feelings that teacher heard the announcement!

"A blessed ray of sunlight after a long night of clouds," Mr. Hammond said, lingering and clasping the superintendent's hand in a hearty grasp. "Tell me what teacher have we whose faith and prayers have reached up to this effort."

"Miss Parkhurst," Mr. Newton said briefly.

"Miss Parkhurst!" echoed Mr. Hammond, in utter amazement, and neither gentleman spoke another word.

To this day Miss Parkhurst has a very indistinct and confused idea as to how she employed the remainder of that half hour, as regards the lesson. But she remembers that she decided that it would not do to resign her class on that Sunday, at least.

15

SATAN AT WORK

There was a very curious combination of circumstances that led to the coming of some of the class to the Saturday prayer meeting. Certain it is that some of them, who had not the slightest idea of being found there, went. Let me tell you how it went and see if you do not think that Satan himself assisted materially in the success of this new enterprise. Of course it was a blunder on his part. It is no new business for him to have a hand even in a prayer meeting, but I think he rarely makes such a bungle for himself as this proved to be.

At their breakfast table on Saturday morning, Mrs. Horton said:

"Girls, this would be as good an evening as any for your croquet party."

Miss Fanny shook her head.

"No, Mother, Miss Parkhurst couldn't come this evening, and you know she invited us to hers; so we will have to wait until we are positive that she has no engagement."

"What engagement has she for the evening that you happen to know about? Oh! I remember; little Nell told of a prayer meeting that was announced at her house. I thought the child must be mistaken and was going to ask you about it, but it slipped my mind. What does it mean?"

"It is true, Mamma, there is a ladies' prayer meeting appointed at her house for this evening, and she is to be the leader."

Young Wells Horton looked up suddenly from the morning paper over which he was glancing while he sipped his coffee.

"Is that an actual fact?" he asked at last, a curious expression on his face and a laugh in his voice.

"A positive fact, Wells; I heard the appointment with my own ears."

Then Mr. Wells Horton leaned back in his chair and indulged in a hearty ha! ha!

"It is the richest thing of the season!" he said at last. "Why I should as soon expect to hear of my Ettie leading a prayer meeting. Mother, you know the hop we attended last Saturday evening, and which scandalized you a little, being on Saturday. Well, Miss Parkhurst was there, and among the last to take her departure, and she was one of the gayest of the party the entire evening. From a dance to a prayer meeting, and leader of both, is quite a jump, I should say."

May Horton came to the rescue.

"She was smuggled into it, as much against her will as it would have been against mine. That absurd Sarah Blake has been sick, and frightened to death because she thought she was going to die, and she seems to think that is an excuse for doing all sorts of absurd and out-of-place things. Miss Parkhurst was just forced into an absurd position. I feel sorry for her."

Her sister, Fanny, spoke almost fiercely.

"I am not sorry for her in the least. Why does she want to pretend to be what she isn't? She has put herself in a false position, and I don't care how much embarrassment it causes her. I don't believe she is any more of a Christian than I am. And she has herself to thank for the attempt to pull two ways at once."

"Judge not that ye —" began Mrs. Horton, who had a character as a Christian to sustain and did not care to have it probed. But her son interrupted her with another laugh.

"This is rich!" he said, when the laugh was over. "I wish gentlemen were admitted. I would like to see Cora Parkhurst in such a position. I tell you what, girls, if you will go and give us a report of it, I will make you a present of a box of kids, assorted colors."

May looked up eagerly.

"Honestly, will you?" she asked.

"As sure as my name is Horton."

"I wouldn't," began Mrs. Horton faintly. "You shouldn't ridicule such things."

"But, Mother," Wells said, "I should think it would be no more than courteous to attend. Of course she ought to be sustained by her class. Come, Fanny, what do you say?"

"It is a horrid bore," Fanny said fretfully. "I should think you might give us the gloves with such disagreeable conditions."

"Not a bit of it," her brother said promptly. "You fulfill the conditions and I furnish the reward; that is fair."

May's eyes were dancing.

"Come, Fanny, let's go," she said. "I would really like to see how she gets out of it."

Fanny's eyes expressed scorn.

"I thought you were sorry for her," she said sharply.

"Well, so I am; but I did not get her into this scrape; she got herself there, by your own showing, and it will not hurt her for us to see what she does. Besides, we really need new gloves, you know, to match our suits."

In this way Satan sent them to the meeting. His arrangements with Miss Celia Evans were conducted on a different scale. She and Lester St. John walked from the post office together on the afternoon of the meeting. "Isn't that a new departure for Miss Parkhurst?" he said, as they passed her door. "I was so amazed to hear that notice last Sunday. If it had been a concert or a dance, it wouldn't have been so surprising. What is the object, anyway? In some classes there would have been a show of sense in it. But she hasn't a scholar to sustain her, has she? At least not more than one."

"How do you know but I am going myself?"

There were reasons why Lester St. John's treatment of this question annoyed his companion. He threw back his head and laughed as loudly as Wells Horton had done.

"I should as soon think of seeing Judge Willard in a prayer meeting!" he said with emphasis.

"Or yourself," she answered, more and more annoyed.

"Myself! Oh yes, sooner. I went to a

prayer meeting not long ago, to please Mr. Hammond; but he is a different sort of teacher from yours."

"Your powers of penetration are remarkable, but it is just possible that you may be disappointed once."

Miss Evans's tone was decidedly spicy. St. John looked at her curiously.

"Now, confess," he said, "that you haven't the most remote intention of going to that meeting tonight. On your honor."

She was silent for a whole second, and in that second of time she had come to a sudden determination, entirely foreign to her previous plans.

"On my honor, then, as you put it in that courteous manner, it is my full intention to be present at that prayer meeting this evening. You are not absolute as an oracle, Mr. St. John."

Now, I want to know if Satan didn't work valiantly for the success of Sarah Blake's idea!

Miss Parkhurst, sitting in her pleasant back parlor in an absolute tremor of excitement and bewilderment as to how all this would end, was actually on the verge of giving him the credit when the gate clicked and a glance out revealed the Hortons coming up the walk and Celia

Evans in the act of crossing the street, opposite the gate; so dismayed was she at this unlooked-for addition to their number. Sarah and Hattie Taylor had been there for five minutes, and she had begun to hope that that would be the extent of their number. As for Hattie, her face was radiant with delight when she saw the girls and realized that they were coming to the meeting.

"Miss Parkhurst," Sarah said, "isn't that so much more than we expected?"

Miss Parkhurst felt that it was so.

"You mustn't depend upon me," she said, in a frightened way. "I really never was at a ladies' prayer meeting in my life. I don't know in the least how they do it. Hattie, you know all about it and can take the lead yourself."

But Hattie was young and timid. Her face flushed painfully.

"I am going to try to help," she said, "but I think we must depend on you."

And by that time the girls were all present and sat in silence, looking at her. It was well she knew nothing about that box of gloves. It would not have tended to compose her thoughts.

At this embarrassing moment, Mr. Tracy's quick step was heard on the walk.

She knew it well, and she caught her breath nervously. Would the girl have sense enough to say that she was engaged? Of course not, since she had lacked the courage to tell her the nature of her engagement. She went to see Mr. Tracy.

"Isn't this a lovely evening?" he said. "I am fortunate in finding you. I want you to go for a walk. It is a surprise to you to have a call from me on Saturday evening, is it not? Make haste, please, I have a scheme in view which will require time."

Now, Mr. Tracy was another whom she had failed to tell of her engagement. She had relied on the almost certainty of his being detained by the pressure of Saturday accounts, and her teeth actually chattered as she realized the necessity of speaking plainly now.

He looked at her in absolute bewilderment and repeated her words mechanically:

"A prayer meeting at your house with your class! Is the whole world growing demented, I wonder?"

Then he turned abruptly, without so much as a farewell bow, and walked away.

Miss Parkhurst went back to her class. "Girls!" she said, speaking fast and nervously. "I don't know what you will think of me, and I can't help it, anyway. I can't lead your meeting this evening. I don't know how to pray. I don't think I ever knew. I have spent a dreadful day. I haven't been the right kind of a Christian. I have been a miserable teacher and a miserable leader in every way. I have felt this for a long time; now I know it. The most I can do is to ask you to pray for me. If anyone in this world ever needed praying for, it is I." And then her voice and words forsook her, and she sobbed aloud.

There are few such prayer meetings as that was. Sarah Blake prayed as one who had learned of the Spirit himself, for you remember she had had no other teacher. And Hattie Taylor prayed from the very depths of her earnest heart, and Miss Parkhurst prayed; she could not help it. She felt so very miserable and longed to get away from that misery; she had been so long tossed about with an unrestful spirit that she cried out with tears to be released. The very last attempt of Satan to discomfort her still more, by sending Mr. Tracy just then, only served to make her feel her loneliness and misery, for she felt that she had offended him and was indeed alone. When her almost despairing cry for help was ended, May Horton, with her usually bright, laughing face very grave, and with tears in her eyes, said:

"I wish you would pray for me. I don't think I ever cared in the least to be a Christian before, but now I almost think I want to be one."

How many boxes of gloves, in his astonishment, would her brother, Wells, have pledged if he could have heard that!

They went out very quietly from that meeting, until Sarah Blake was left alone with her weeping teacher.

"Don't let me keep you, Sarah," she said, looking up as she realized that the others were gone. "I hope you will all forgive me for making your meeting a failure, but I was so very wretched I couldn't help it. You don't know the misery that I have lived through, ever since that awful night at your house, when I found that I didn't know how to pray I don't think I have seen a happy moment since. But I haven't meant to be a hypocrite, indeed I haven't; I thought I meant it."

"You are not a hypocrite," Sarah said, her tones almost those of indignation, as if her teacher had received a slight. "Do you think a hypocrite could have showed me the way to Jesus? Oh, Miss Parkhurst, doesn't that comfort you, that you saved one soul for Christ? I think I could live a lifetime for that."

"Sarah," said Miss Parkhurst, one of those determined looks settling on her face, which those who knew her well recognized as a token that something was settled, "let us kneel down here again and you pray for me. I will have this question settled; I will not live in this way another hour; I don't know whether I was ever a Christian in my life or not, but I mean to be; I mean to begin this minute. Now, show me the way; pray for me, just as you did for yourself when you were in that horror that you told about. I am sure I have been in horror a long time, if anyone ever was."

It was almost an hour after that, that teacher and pupil left the back parlor and walked down the hall together.

Those who knew Miss Parkhurst best would hardly at the first glance, have recognized her face — it was aglow with a new feeling.

"Thank you," she said, pressing Sarah's hand. "Thank you more than words can tell. I know now what you meant when you expressed thanks to me, when you thought I had helped you."

"You did help me," Sarah said, as decidedly as before. "You gave me help that I shall never forget, here or in heaven."

"That is just it; you have given me just that kind of help tonight; it is not to be forgotten. Good-bye; I shall see you tomorrow. I shall be a different teacher from what you ever had in me before."

Do you imagine that Satan ever did a more grievous piece of work for himself than when he took the ordering of that prayer meeting into his own hands? There was work done that evening that shall tell against him, in far-reaching influences, throughout all eternity.

16

THE RESULT OF THE WORK

I do not know that I can tell you much about that Sunday morning — what it was to Miss Parkhurst, I mean. You have heard people in prayer meeting tell about how different the world looked after their conversion, have you not? Miss Parkhurst had heard such expressions a great many times, and she had not understood them. The whole force of their meaning burst upon her that morning.

She was early to her seat and welcomed the girls with a glad smile.

"I haven't the least idea how to teach you," she said. "I don't think it has been teaching at all that I have done. I propose that we all begin again. I don't want to leave you, and I feel sure that you don't want to leave me. So let us all be scholars and all teachers. I'll study my lesson as hard as I can, and you do the same, then whatever we get out of them we will each give to the others. Shall that be the way?"

It was a kind of teaching that was new enough to the girls, but it seemed, from its very newness, to please their fancy, and they gave themselves to the work in hand with an interest that drew the attention of the class next to them and quieted the restlessness of even Larry Bates.

They did not adhere to the text of the lesson very closely. The teacher had not learned how to hinge the thoughts in her heart to the text before her, so she broke off suddenly:

"I want to talk to you about something, girls. What can we do now for each other? I want to do something for you and for Christ, and I don't in the least know how to go to work. Do any of you know something that we can do?"

It was an embarrassing way to talk; at least, it embarrassed some of them. She acted precisely as if they were all Christians, and the obligation to work rested as much on one as another, so Celia and the Horton girls, who were generally foremost to express their views, maintained an embarrassed silence, and Hattie, the quietest of their number, had her word to say.

"There is one thing, Miss Parkhurst, that I have thought about a great deal."

Miss Parkhurst turned eagerly:

"Tell us what it is, Hattie; your eyes have been open while I have been asleep; perhaps you are just the one to help us."

"No, it is you who are to help us," Hattie said with a naive laugh. "You have not been to the prayer meeting very much this summer, have you?"

"No, but I am going," Miss Parkhurst said quickly. "I have thought of that myself."

"Well, this is what I am thinking: Can't something be done to make them more interesting? You can't think how dull they are. I didn't notice it so much until Sarah began to come, and then when I wanted them to be interesting for her sake, I found that they were very stupid indeed."

"They are," chimed in Sarah. "I thought, of course, I should enjoy a meeting, just because it was a meeting, but I find there must be something to enjoy before we can enjoy it, even if it is in a church building."

Miss Parkhurst looked perplexed.

"I know they are very dull," she said musingly. "Once a friend, who is not a Christian, went with me, and when we came out, he said he thought an hour in state prison would be pleasanter than that. But I thought it was because he had no interest. But, now that you speak of it, it really seems as if no one had much interest. Still, I'm sure I don't know what we could do to better the matter, except to go. That would be a help, as far as it goes. Suppose we all make an engagement to meet each other at Thursday-evening meeting and let nothing interfere with that promise except such a reason as would interfere with a music lesson, say, if we were taking lessons."

This was certainly putting the standard rather low, religion on a level with music lessons. And yet it was very high compared with the way in which it is generally looked upon, and Miss Parkhurst was so accustomed to the general way of looking at such things that it seemed to her a step in advance. She noticed that Sarah still looked grave.

"Wouldn't that be a good way to do?" she asked, addressing them all, and looking at Sarah.

"Excellent, as far as it goes," Sarah said, with a little laugh. "But what troubles me is, how can we make it helpful to us and to others when we get there? If we had better singing, I think it would be a help."

"So it would," Miss Parkhurst said, with brightening eyes. "I begin to see light. Fanny, your voice and May's would be a real miracle in that meeting. You will both go, and both sing, won't you?"

May laughed a little.

"Why, Miss Parkhurst," she said, "Fanny and I are not Christians. We actually never went to prayer meeting in our lives. What would the people think to see us come in?"

As to that, Miss Parkhurst said she did not think it would seem any more strange to see them there than it would to see many church members, herself among the number. She was ashamed and frightened the other evening to think that she had been so seldom.

The end of all the talk was that, with many excuses and some laughter, the entire class engaged to meet each other at the next Thursday-evening meeting.

"In the meantime," Miss Parkhurst said, "I mean to think of this matter and see if there is anything more that we can do. If any of you get some light in the matter, I wish you would let me know."

With this thought in mind, she went directly to Mr. Hammond at the close of the session and said abruptly, "I wonder if you can help us?" and then she told the subject of their thoughts.

"At the Salem Street Church, the ladies have a word to say in the social prayer meetings, equally with the gentlemen," Mr. Hammond said, and in his voice there was a respectful ring, such as he had never given to her before. There was a change in Miss Parkhurst's line of action: It commanded the respect of a working Christian.

As for the lady, she stood looking up at him in a dazed sort of way. It was not possible that the reference to the Salem Street Church could have anything to do with them. And yet he waited for her to answer.

"You do not mean," she said at last, and there was a little catching of her breath as if the idea actually alarmed her, "You do not mean that we could do that!"

"Why not?"

"Why, because it is not done in our church."

"In our church the meetings for prayer are not well attended; should we therefore not go?"

"But it is not quite the thing, is it?"

"Why not?"

"Isn't it out of place?"

"Why?"

Miss Parkhurst laughed.

"You have a very queer way of asking questions, Mr. Hammond. But it has always been considered so; now, hasn't it?"

"Not by me."

"Do you really like to hear ladies take part in meetings?"

"May I ask you another question before I answer yours? When I attend the sewing society and meet fifty ladies and gentlemen, do you suppose I like to hear Mrs. Banks tell of her proposed trip to Europe and the route she designs taking?"

"Why, I daresay you do. At least, I enjoy hearing her, for it is just the journey that I want to take, and mean to, if I ever get a chance, and anything concerning it always interests me."

"You have touched the exact point. Now, I have a desire to go to heaven, and I mean to go there, and anything said on the subject as to difficulties to be avoided or dangers to be shunned, I am anxious to hear about; anything that you can say concerning that journey will deeply interest me. Now, you know our society meets in the chapel, and so does our prayer meeting, the only difference being that we rarely have the good fortune to number at our prayer meeting as many as gather at the societies. The question with me is, why should not Mrs. Banks tell us of a word connected with the other Journey, in which we agree all are supposed to be interested, as well as of that journey to Europe?"

"What makes people feel so different about the two things?"

"I am sure I do not know; the force of education and habit, perhaps."

"But how came people to be so educated? It seems as if such a universal habit must have a foundation."

"How came it to be so easy to get a large company of Christians together to enjoy our society rehearsals, and so few to our prayer meetings? Must not so universal a custom as that have a foundation in right?"

Then Miss Parkhurst laughed again.

"You keep getting me in tight places," she said pleasantly. "These are all new thoughts to me, but it does look queer, as though something, somewhere, was wrong. I want to tell you, Mr. Hammond, that I am thoroughly in earnest. I don't know whether I ever was or not; I have stopped trying to find out; but I know I am now, and just as fast as I find out what there is to do, I mean to try to do it. It almost takes my breath away to think of taking a part in meeting. I have always had very fixed ideas about those things; at least, I thought I had; but I mean to look at them, and if they really have no foundation, why, they can't be leaned upon, that is all. I have ever so much work to undo; I wish you would help me, Mr. Hammond, whenever you can. These girls actually lean on me, and I have led them in very queer ways. I shall have to work hard and at a great disadvantage, so I need all the help I can get."

She went away and left Mr. Hammond grave and thoughtful. The subject of his thought was this: "She has just roused to a sense of the importance of living. How heartily she is going to work. I profess to have had an idea of its solemnity and responsibility these many years. Do I work with the will that she is bringing even now?"

Miss Parkhurst, as she went down Chestnut Street, said:

"Oh, my patience!" It was her favorite exclamation, and she had not yet broken herself of its use. "I wonder if it is possible that it can be my duty to do that! I never could do it in the world, and yet I am not naturally timid. They say I make an unusually good secretary for the society because my voice does not tremble when I read the reports. I wonder what makes me feel so about the other thing? I mean to think about it. What a world of things there are to think about, and I have never done any of it before! But I am willing to think, now that the horrible feeling that has been gnawing for months has gone. I wonder what George will say?" And there came a

218

little twinge of doubt and pain.

So the leaven of Satan's precious interference was working. Little he wot of what he wrought by one hour's interference. Neither did the first fruits end here.

Naturally, Mr. Wells Horton inquired as to the result of the wager. He was not at home in the meeting. Satan arranged that, too, by taking him to the theater the evening before, and thence home with a friend, as he did not meet the girls until after the added influence of the Sunday school was upon them. Then he was astonished and puzzled at the answer.

"You may keep the gloves," Fanny said, and there was either irritation or decision in her voice, and he didn't know which. "We had a good meeting. I never liked and respected Miss Parkhurst so much in my life. You may know I did, for I promised to go to the Thursday-evening prayer meeting this week, just because she wanted us to, and so has May. So it isn't likely you will get an account of the meeting from us, such as you want."

"The Millennium or something must be coming," Wells said. But he sent up the box of gloves and thought about the matter several times that day.

"She has gone to work for our own

meeting," Mr. Hammond said on his way home. "That is a good hint, certainly. If the girls help sing, there will be more interest than usual. I wonder if I can get my boys to go? I shall try, at least. I mean to get Lewis to unite with me in making this whole matter a subject of special prayer."

17

NEW WORKMEN

The three men and five women who always went to Harvard Street prayer meeting were all in their places, and it was just time to open the meeting, when the opening door admitted half a dozen more of the occasional comers — that class who go to the weekly prayer meeting when it is pleasant, when it is not too warm, when they have no other and more important engagement, such as a concert or an evening party, or it may be a chance caller.

Miss Parkhurst did not even belong to this class; in that her engagement and detentions were the constant rule, and her comings the exception. Nevertheless, after the half dozen or so, came she. A small feeling of surprise seemed to pass through the mind of every lady present; they had thought the evening too pleasant for her. But the very next opening of the door revealed to their astonished eyes a wonder. There were Fanny and May Horton and their brother, Wells! Could anything be more amazing than that! Those three, who had never been known to be in a prayer meeting in their lives, at least on a weekday evening, to appear at once, was almost too much for the curiosity of the constant attendees. They knew nothing about the promise, you know, of the Sunday before, so they could only stare and wonder.

This was the way that Wells happened to be of the number:

"Girls," he said, meeting them as they went shyly out the back piazza, feeling someway very foolish over their promise, "girls, what will you take to let me go with you this evening?"

They both stopped and looked at him.

"You!" Fanny said at last, in utter amazement, then she recovered herself. "Now, Wells Horton, you aren't going to do any such thing. A married man like you ought to be above such baby lowness as disturbing a prayer meeting. I shall have nothing to do with it, and you needn't think it."

Wells laughed.

"What a little firerocket you are, Fanny," he said, good-humoredly. "I haven't the least idea of disturbing the meeting. Why should I take that trouble? Besides, I have too much respect for Mother. I'll tell you the solitary motive I have — it is curiosity; something happened downtown today that made me curious, and I want to investigate; the prayer meeting is the best place I can think of to help me in it; and if I go with you, it will only look as though I went to take care of you, as I am in duty bound to do; so where's the harm? Etta isn't at home, you know, and a fellow must do something."

"What happened to arouse your curiosity to such a degree?" May asked him, but he shook his head.

"That would be a breach of confidence," he said. "But as it had to do with Tracy and Cora Parkhurst, I don't mind telling you that."

"Well, come on," May said. "We shall be late and create more of a sensation than is necessary. It is no very wonderful thing, anyway. Other people have been even to such strange places as prayer meetings before and kept their identity."

By the time Miss Parkhurst's entire class had gathered about her, the surprise had grown and spread over every face. That Mr. Hammond would presently enter with his train of boys was surprising, too. But it was not overpowering; he had accomplished that feat before, not many times, it is true, and everyone there knew that they came because Mr. Hammond wanted them to, and for no other earthly reason. Still, it was something utterly new. But when the door opened for the last time — opened with a creak and closed with a bang, as if someone who came decided in haste and wanted it over with, when that someone who walked with resolute step to the very second seat from the desk and looked about him with an almost defiant air, proved to be Mr. Tracy himself — then the surprise and excitement almost overflowed into audible sounds.

During these comings Mr. Gordon had been reading a chapter in the Bible — reading it with blurred eyes and a somewhat choked voice. He was very glad to see his son there; but a father may perhaps be pardoned for having a little sore, bewildered feeling at his heart when he realized how little influence his wishes have over a son and what a powerful influence some other mind exerts over him. But Mr. Gordon did not fail to remember and be thankful, then and there, that the man who was exerting the influence was Mr. Hammond, and that the influence was what it was. The chapter was concluded, and the usual long, drawn-out prayer followed, made always by the same old man, who talked too low to be heard. Then Mr. Gordon gave out a hymn. Now, the singing that they had at the Harvard Street prayer meeting was something to be remembered. It so happened that not a single constant attendee was a singer. Mr. Hammond sang a heavy bass, but he could better have preached a sermon than started a tune, so the reading fell to the lot of the old gentleman aforesaid; not a lot that he coveted by any means, but a position that the good old man, with his cracked and trembling voice, accepted as a cross. So they generally quavered through "China" or "Balerma" or "Ortonville" as best they could, and they were sure to be keyed either too high or too low. As Mr. Baker, with unusual hesitation, fumbled through his book for a tune and usually alighted on "Martyn," it suddenly occurred to Miss Parkhurst that it was a very strange thing that she, with her voice, had thought that her sole work or duty on the rare occasions when she had been at prayer meeting was to keep from laughter over Mr. Baker's music. In his unusual perturbation, he did worse than ever, and the first line of "Martyn" was wailed out in so high a key that before the second part of the tune was reached, it ended in ominous silence. Miss Parkhurst leaned forward with a beseeching nod at Fanny Horton. Now the entire Horton family were musical geniuses, so fond of music that they seemed to *have* to sing whenever there was opportunity. But this was an entirely new place for their voices to be heard, and whether they would respond to the occasion was much to be doubted. Neither she nor his sisters were prepared for the splendid voice which suddenly took up old "Martyn." In fact, it may be questioned whether Mr. Wells Horton was not surprised at himself. But how grandly that hymn rolled through the astonished aisles! Fanny and May Horton took it up with a will, so also did Miss Parkhurst, and the boys in Mr. Hammond's set, after one or two comical glances around the room, gave themselves up to the enjoyment of the occasion and sang, too. What an inspiration that hymn was! It seemed to wake everybody up. There was a thrill in Mr. Gordon's voice, as he commented on one of the verses in the chapter read, that sounded as though he had been encouraged. But the singing is not the entire life of a prayer meeting. There came very early in the evening one of those long, and, to anxious hearts, fearful pauses, that are given to overtaking a meeting, where the burden of the work rests on the minister, and which are found nowhere else on earth save in a social prayer meeting.

I wish I could explain to you the tumult in which Miss Parkhurst had been since Sabbath. It was not like that other tumult in which heart and soul and brain whirled together, and life was miserable. This time, high up and grand, the soul rested in the consciousness of an awakened and assured love and trust, and a feeling that whatever was right for her to do she meant to do. Still, it was nervous work, this thinking. Mr. Hammond had such queer ideas. Why, as far back as the oldest of them could remember, the women of Harvard Street Church had obeyed the Pauline injunction and kept silent. Unless, indeed, one excepted the society meetings and the meetings for the discussion of picnics or not picnics, and other objects of that nature; meetings held, to be sure, in this same chapel, under such circumstances, how the ladies *had* talked. But that was different, to be sure; and yet Miss Parkhurst's awakened and honest conscience tried in vain to explain to herself just the point of difference.

"It *is* different, though," she said, stoutly. "Of course it is. Mr. Hammond may say what he likes, it is the business of the gentlemen to take the time in a social prayer meeting. They have always done it, and they know how, and that is more than I do. What in the world could I say that would be worth listening to? Of course I have something to say at the society meetings, for I am the secretary and know all about the work and the business."

This she told herself in the quiet of her own room at home and almost settled the question with that half conscious undertone of possibility that the honest doubter always leaves, that if she should be shown that her position was wrong, she would think it over again. It is nearly sure to be those who are determined *not* to be convinced who are entirely positive on questions like these. Now she was in the prayer meeting, and the gentlemen who should occupy the time were not doing it. The few representatives who always did their share had done it, and she was not even here willing to admit that it would be the edifying thing in the world that they should do it over again, or take up more of the time. Yet, here they were sitting and staring at the floor and the ceiling, the minister nervously opening and shutting his hymnbook, and saying at stated intervals, "I hope you will not let the time run to waste, brethren."

Mr. Tracy sat where she could get a side view of his face, and there was a sarcastic smile, almost a sneer, spreading over it. And the "brethren" sat in solemn silence. There were a few present, members of the church, who had not taken part, but they rarely did. Doubtless they thought that they could not speak to "edification" — that it would be altogether more profitable to spend the time that they would occupy in staring at the floor.

"Why *can't* Mr. Hammond say something?" Miss Parkhurst said to herself in a heat, and almost in vexation. Yet, what would she have him say? With the first invitation of the pastor, "Will some brother lead in prayer?" he had responded promptly, in a short, fervent prayer, and his friend and coworker, Mr. Lewis, had followed. Then when the invitation was given to speak a word, he had spoken just his word, simply, quietly, without rising from his seat, as he might have spoken in her parlor. She knew exactly what he said.

" 'Ye are my witnesses, saith the Lord.' I witness tonight that he is faithful who promised. I have had a proof of his faithfulness today."

Just this sentence, spoken in so natural a tone that Miss Parkhurst could almost imagine herself forgetting that it was a meeting in the church and asking him to tell them about his proof exactly as she would have done had he been speaking to her. She wondered why Mr. Gordon did not do it, and said that if she were a minister, she would. And I want to say in passing that, in my opinion, if Mr. Gordon had done just that, they would have had a great deal better prayer meeting.

Still they sat and looked, until the silence was becoming horrible to some and ludicrous to others. Mr. Gordon at last broke the awfulness by asking them to sing, "One more day's work for Jesus." This, of itself, was an invitation; he knew that the Hortons could sing it, and his heart yearned for something like naturalness and sweetness in the prayer meeting, though he did not understand how to bring it about.

They sang it, only Miss Parkhurst stopped suddenly after the line, "How sweet the work has been," and she knew by the dull thuds that her heart was giving that she had made up her mind.

"I haven't worked for him in the least

today," she said, the instant the singing ceased. "I don't think I have done one single thing to tell anyone about him, but I want to, and oh, I mean to — I mean to try."

Did you ever sit in the oppressive stillness of an August evening, feeling as if all sounds in earth and air had forever ceased, until you suddenly heard the quick, loud, majestic rolls of thunder? And do you remember how you were startled? Certainly Miss Parkhurst's voice was not like thunder — it was low and tremulous — but not peal on peal of thunder that would shake the church could have startled the Harvard Street people like that low voice. The very air seemed to rustle, and the starers left the floor and ceiling and stared at the owner of that courageous voice.

Mr. Hammond, as I have said, found it nearly impossible to lead a hymn. But impossible things can sometimes be done, and almost as soon as the voice stopped, he sang that solemn old hymn, "Now I resolve with all my heart and all my powers to serve the Lord!"

The spell was broken. Hattie Taylor, ashamed and confused that her teacher, who had begged them to help her, had been left to fight this great struggle alone, said suddenly:

"I am one of his children. I love him."

Then instantly came Sarah Blake with her strong, untrembling voice:

"He found me when I was sick and miserable and afraid, and he gave me rest and peace. *How* I love him I can never tell, but I mean to try to now."

Electric shocks, that is what they were like — quick, sharp, and repeated. The old men leaned forward in their seats and drew their breath in wonder. As for the minister, he wiped the large, salty tears that were falling down his cheek, and would have risen to speak, when there came a sudden and overwhelming surprise to them all:

"I have decided that I want this Friend for my own. Pray for me," said a low, clear, firm voice, that belonged to no one but Lester St. John, the most correct and polite and self-satisfied and hopeless young man in the city, so anyone who knew him would have said; yet, there was a sound in his voice that said, "I mean it."

"Let us pray," said Mr. Hammond, and if you remember that this young man was in his Sabbath-school class, and that he had been praying and working for him for over four years, you will know all about that prayer that words can tell.

They went out very slowly from that

meeting. The excitement was too intense for sound. Only Mr. Hammond grasped Miss Parkhurst's hand as she passed, with unusual meaning in the simple "good night." But Mr. Tracy was right behind him and drew the hand within his arm with an authoritative air, and his first words were, before they had hardly passed out of the hearing of the others:

"Cora, have you taken leave of your senses, or what *is* the meaning of this remarkable scene?"

18

UNEXPECTED WORK

Now I take it that no lady enjoys being addressed in quite the tone that Mr. Tracy used to his companion that evening, even though she is engaged to marry him at some future day. She was a good deal startled, for it was not his usual manner of address; she had expected a sort of good-natured ridicule — sarcasm that appeared courteous, if there is such a thing, and yet that had a sting in it. She was not prepared for the stern, excited, almost angry, tone and the contemptuous manner. It is a pity he had not known, if his motive was a desire to influence her in the future, that he had chosen quite the wrong way.

She had come out from the meeting excited, it is true, but at the same time somewhat shamefaced. She was already beginning to experience that reaction of feeling which questions whether, after all, one has not been doing a very foolish thing. She had by no means enjoyed the new duty so much that she was not half longing to be told that the idea of its being *duty* was utterly a mistake, and under the influence of this reaction was more than half ready to promise that she could not be so led away again. But not if she were asked in that tone.

One thing she knew, that whether it was a duty or not to do as she had done, it was that motive and that alone which prompted her. She might have been mistaken — she was willing, and, as I said, almost anxious to think so; but such being her motive, it was worthy of respect and kind treatment. She was hurt by his tone and words, and she was, by a method of reasoning not understood by herself, at once convinced that she had, at least, done nothing wrong, but she was not angry. Her religious experience had been too real and too recent to admit of such a feeling. Besides, amid all the tumult of self-questioning and excitement that the evening had brought forth, there had been the realization of a present, loving, listening Savior that had lifted her out of herself. She answered him gently but more decidedly than she would have done had his words been different.

"Why, George, what a strange way to speak to me! I have surely done nothing so very wonderful."

"Something wonderfully foolish," he said, in increased annoyance, her quiet tone seeming to have the wrong effect. There is something strange about it, perhaps, but it is certainly true that human nature would almost rather be called wicked than foolish. Something of this feeling stirred in Miss Parkhurst's mind as she answered, still in a kindly tone, but with the least touch of dignity:

"If that is the case, I have only to answer to myself for it."

"In that I should differ with you," he said quickly. "I think you have someone else to answer to, one who is supposed to be interested in what you say and do, and who by no means approves of your doing conspicuous and absurd things."

If they had been talking at cross-purposes, they could not have got on better than they did this evening. Miss Parkhurst hardly heard the last half of his sentence; the first of it stirred in her heart those new and inexpressibly sweet thoughts that she really was not her own but had been bought with a price.

"I should not have said that," she answered him, and her voice was sweet and low. "There is One to whom I am accountable. I realize it now as I never did before, and, George, I have wanted to have a little talk with you about it. I am glad that this has called it forth. Things are very different with me from what they were."

Mr. Tracy had certainly lost his usual deferential manner. He interrupted her, almost rudely:

"Cora, I beg that you will spare me all cant this evening. I am not in the mood for it, and it does not become you. I cannot imagine why you should take it up. I want to talk a little common sense. Was it a wager or a philopena, or what in the canopy did influence you?"

There are things that are very hard to bear. In the first flush of her new trust and love, it was hard for Miss Parkhurst to hear the sharp, stinging words, especially hard to hear them from his lips.

"George, don't talk so," she said, and her tone was pleading. "You don't know what you are saying. I don't wonder that you are surprised. Indeed, it isn't strange that you are a little hurt, it came so suddenly upon you. I certainly should have told you if I had known before what I was to do. But, George, I couldn't help it. He saw it plainly to be my duty; nothing was ever plainer to me."

"Nonsense!" he said, growing more

vexed every moment. "Why will you insist in wasting that sort of talk on me? You ought to know that I am not the one to endure it. I understand very plainly what all this amounts to. It is just the influence of that fanatic fool, Hammond. I have seen the working of it for some time, though you and he both acted as if you thought I was blind. I, for one, don't thank him for his meddling. It looks to me like anything but the Christian spirit that he is always canting about. Confound the fellow! I could shoot him for his insufferable impudence."

Miss Parkhurst was very rarely angry with anyone; her nature had in that respect been almost perfect. But that class of people, when they are aroused, are generally very angry indeed. She withdrew her hand from Mr. Tracy's arm, and she had decidedly the advantage of him in that her voice was low-toned and her manner quiet.

"Mr. Tracy, no degree of intimacy warrants the use of such language as you have compelled me to hear. I have endured hints of that sort from your lips before, without telling you what I thought, that they were unkind and ungentlemanly; but you have certainly gone too far, and I shall have to ask you to apologize before I can feel that you are the friend to me that you have professed to be."

Mr. Tracy's anger was roused to a white heat. He seemed to neither know, nor care, what he said.

"I will never apologize!" he said, speaking louder than was wise, considering it was a public street, and there were many people passing. "I will never apologize! I consider it is you who owe an apology to me. You have made yourself conspicuous in a very offensive way, and that, in view of your position, and your connection with me, and knowing my views, you had no right to do."

Then they walked the length of half a block without speaking. When Miss Parkhurst broke the silence, her voice had so changed that it frightened herself.

"Mr. Tracy, I am very sorry I have disgraced you; I had not the slightest intention of doing anything to offend, or to hurt your feelings. Indeed, I scarcely thought of you this evening at all; I believed, and I still believe, that there was Another to please whose claims come before yours or any human being's. I am unfortunate, it seems, in my attempts to explanation, as we seem to get farther apart every moment. Perhaps it will be well to think the matter over quietly, without doing any more talking, and in order to relieve you from the necessity of saying anything further to me, as I am right at Uncle Harmon's door, I will step in there, and Cousin Lawrence can see me home."

In less time than it takes me to tell it, Mr. Tracy found himself alone with his anger on a brightly lighted street some distance from home.

I want to make some excuse for this young man, if I can. He was not habitually rude and unfeeling; indeed, his usual manner was the very reverse of this; he was almost amazed at himself, even in his blind anger, which prevented his reasoning clearly as to what had happened. He was not a passionate man, either, and perhaps the anger had him at a greater disadvantage for the moment, even on this account.

You have doubtless discovered long ago what Miss Parkhurst ought to have realized before she engaged herself to him, that he had very little sympathy with Christianity in any form. At the same time, it had heretofore had very little to do with his life; it had not run athwart a single plan of his, and very lately, although he had all his life associated with so-called Christian people, I hardly think he was to blame for his often-expressed opinion that there was too little difference between the church and the world to distinguish with the naked eye which specimen was before you. His lack of sympathy had hitherto exhausted itself in good-natured raillery, and so had been comparatively harmless.

But it so happened that he held very positive views as to "woman's sphere," "woman's duties," and the like; he was entirely willing to grant a lady even an intimate friend of his, the privilege of dancing all the evening with whomsoever she chose, and that meant with whomever she chanced to have a passing introduction. But he had stoutly declared that no lady friend of his could so forget her position and what was due to society as to appear before the public and make a speech to a promiscuous assembly. He meant, of course, a prayer meeting, for he had no sort of objection to quite public remarks in the aforesaid dancing party.

He had been so unwise or so unfortunate as to get into a discussion of this sort on the very day of which I write, the question having been introduced by the quotation of some remark made by Mr. Hammond. So Mr. Tracy, in addition to his natural aversion to such exhibitions, had the added inducement of differing emphatically from Mr. Hammond's views, a duty which was an absolute pleasure to him, and which he never neglected. To him the justice to understand that the idea of his promised wife being brought into conflict with him on this point was a thought which never for one moment occurred to him.

One of the disputants proved to be Mr. Wells Horton, and that gentleman, having gleaned from various sources that strange transformations were going on in Miss Parkhurst's class, kept his own counsel as to names but volunteered the opinion that he, Mr. Tracy, would have the pleasure of listening to the voices of some of his lady friends that very evening, if he would go to the Harvard Street Church.

Mr. Tracy ran over rapidly in his mind his list of lady friends who were in the habit of frequenting Harvard Street prayer meeting. They were few, and it did not take him long, and so assured was he of their oneness of feeling, that Miss Parkhurst's name did not even occur to him in this connection. Why should it? He had heard her express herself much more strongly than he had ever done. So indifferent was he to the ladies whom he decided composed his list of acquaintances in that direction, that he laughingly proposed to Wells to go to the meeting in his company and even proposed to wager that not a lady who had ever received any attentions from him would open her lips.

Perhaps you can imagine his sensation when the first lady's voice to break the silence was that of his promised wife! It may be that this explanation will in a measure excuse his language and manner, when in the full heat of his wounded pride and rage he came in contact with Miss Parkhurst. You must constantly remember that he understood no more the strong forces at work in her heart that produced these results than a machine does. There was only one explanation that suggested itself in his mind, and that was that it was all the work of his enemy, Mr. Hammond. This you will readily understand was the aggravating bitterness that helped to carry his passion beyond control.

I wish I might but faintly tell you of his sensation when he found himself thus suddenly left alone on the street. He walked on rapidly in his blind rage for several minutes before he realized that every step took him farther from home and nearer to Miss Parkhurst's door, where he was liable to be questioned as to what had become of that young lady. He wheeled suddenly and walked fast in the other direction for a moment, until the fear of meeting certain of his acquaintances overcame him.

"What if I should meet that contemptible puppy of a Wells Horton!" he said to himself and failed to see the inconsistency of calling his hitherto intimate friend by such a name. Such friendship, by the way, must be very valuable. He finally turned down a back street, which, by making several turns and crossings, would intersect with Forest Street and so get him home.

19

WORKING IN DARKNESS

You are not to suppose that Miss Parkhurst's state of mind, as she went through the hall to her uncle's sitting-room door, was enviable; indeed, you would have pitied her. Surprise, indignation, and sorrow, all struggled for the mastery. Besides which, she let that troublesome question come in that is nearly certain to intrude, even on heavy anxiety and sorrow. "What will they think of me for coming this evening, and alone?"

Not daring to give herself time to think much about it, she pushed open the door and entered the brightly lighted sitting room, wishing with all her heart that the supply of gas would be suddenly and utterly exhausted.

"Well!" her uncle said, sitting erect and looking surprised, "where in the world did *you* come from at this hour, and where is Tracy?"

Could two more unanswerable questions be invented? They made the blood mount higher on Miss Parkhurst's face, and she stood still, not knowing what to do next. Her aunt was engaged with a lady at the farther end of the room, some private business matter, apparently, for she did not come forward. Larry wasn't there at all, and the gentleman who was talking earnestly with her uncle when she appeared was Mr. Hammond. Now, what was she to do? Quick as thought, there flashed over her the peculiarities of her position, the necessity for making some explanation, the necessity of securing company home, and the impossibility of telling anything that would not reveal the trouble she was in. Above all came the thought, what would George say if he could see her there? She questioned whether in his then state of mind he would not have accused her of having contrived this meeting with Mr. Hammond. It took but an instant for all these confused thoughts to rush through her brain. The next, Mr. Hammond had risen and advanced toward her.

"Good evening again," he said. "Lawrence and I have reached here before you, you see."

"Where is Lawrence?" she asked, catching suddenly at the name that was to have helped her.

"He went directly to his room. He is suffering from a sudden attack of headache. I hope, sir, it will prove to be nothing *but* a headache." This last being addressed to the father.

At this last drop of trouble, added to her exciting evening, Miss Parkhurst lost all vestige of self-control, and said, in a quick, nervous voice, in which there was a sound of tears:

"What in the world shall I do? I don't know how I am to get home!"

"How is that?" said the uncle, leaning forward suddenly. "Get home? Why, where is Tracy? Won't he be in for you?"

"Mr. Bates," said Mr. Hammond, as if a sudden thought had come to him, and as if Miss Parkhurst and her affairs were not of the slightest consequence, "can you step into the office before ten, in the morning? The sooner that business is attended to, the better it will be, perhaps." Then, rising, he turned to Miss Parkhurst:

"If you are going home soon, may I walk down with you?"

"Sure enough," said the uncle, coming out of his chair and standing before her. "He goes right by your house. What did you say had become of Tracy?"

"Good evening, then," Mr. Hammond said, moving toward the door, for Miss

Parkhurst had risen the moment he addressed her, as if it would be a relief to her to get away from those stupid questions, even though she went with him. And yet she took in, in all its bearings, the embarrassments of a walk with Mr. Hammond. What if they should meet George? Or the boys, to laugh over it, and tease him with it the next morning. Besides, what should she say to him — to Mr. Hammond himself? How should she explain the strangeness of her position?

This last need not have troubled her. Mr. Hammond talked just as usual, except, perhaps, that he required only monosyllables from her in answer. He seemed not embarrassed, nor disturbed in any way. In fact, he acted precisely as though he was not aware of anything embarrassing in the circumstances.

They had reached the very steps of her house, and she, meeting not a person that she knew, and given time to think, had grown more quiet, then he said:

"Miss Parkhurst, I do not know whether to speak or be silent; perhaps it would be better to say nothing. And, yes, of course, I know that you are in some discomfort. Perhaps it may not be improper for me to say that I think you have done a work for the cause of the Master this evening that will not stop here, and I believe, whatever annoyance or trial may grow out of it to you, God will cause to work for good."

She turned toward him eyes that were brimming with tears, and said:

"I thank you. I feel that I *do* need a kind word. I am in trouble, and yet I am sure I have done right. That is, I know I have in some things, but I think I may have been undoing some of it since."

"If any lack wisdom, let him ask of God," he said earnestly. He did not want to press her confidence, nor lead her to tell in the first flush of her excitement what she would regret when she had grown more quiet.

He went away at once, and Miss Parkhurst hurried to her room, thankful that her mother had grown weary of waiting for her. That little touch of sympathy had done her good. The tears in her eyes had softened her heart. She began to realize that she might have been at fault. It was cruel, certainly, to leave a gentleman on the street in the unceremonious way that she had done. What were people to suppose who met him? It was placing him in a very unpleasant position — hardly anything could justify it.

"He really has a right to be angry," she

said, and for the time she forgot all the hard things he had said to her and lost herself in pity over his side of the question. This thought grew upon her, until presently she drew pencil and paper to her and began a little note, in the old, familiar way:

DEAR GEORGE:

It was rude and unkind in me to leave you in the way I did. I do not wonder that you were vexed. I do not see what could have made me do it.

Thus far, and then she paused to read it over. You see she utterly ignored the fact that it was not the leaving him that had been the producing cause of the trouble between them. There came dimly to her now the memory of certain words of his, and so she wrote:

I surprised and grieved you tonight. I do not wonder at that, either. It was a very sudden thing for me to do. I ought to have warned you, but how could I, when I hadn't the least idea of such a thing myself? I wish I could explain to you how I felt and what it meant. That is what I should have tried to do, instead of leaving you in a pet, like a spoiled child that I am. Forgive me, please, and I will be good tomorrow when you come to see me. You see, I am taking it for granted that you are going to forgive me and come as usual, and I know you will, for you have endured too much naughtiness from me to punish me now. So I will write myself, as usual,

YOUR CORA.

You would hardly believe how light her heart felt after this note was written and sealed. It seemed to her that the heavy trouble had all been smoothed over. She was not accustomed to careful and continued thought on any subject, you will remember. And now it actually began to seem to her that the great difficulty had been that she, growing tired of his company, had suddenly and rudely deserted him. The episode having come later in the evening had spread itself over the other. She drew a sigh of relief as she laid the note on the table, feeling only sorry that there was no possible way of getting it to the gentleman that night. Then she went to that blessed resort from all care and pain

251

and trouble, and if Mr. Tracy could only have heard himself prayed for, it would surely have calmed his feelings.

He was not having such a quiet closing to this stormy evening. He was in a perfect rage, and the more he thought about the whole affair, the more angry he grew. He sat up till midnight, thinking it over — not thinking, either, the angry and disgusted fancies that floated through his brain can be characterized by no such dignified name as that. Altogether, he will be likely to remember that night, and, for that matter, the day that followed it.

Notwithstanding the late hours of the night before, he wakened early and as he went about his rooms, continued his puzzled, troubled thought. He was decidedly calmer. A few hours of sleep, and the presence of staid and dignified sunlight do much toward quieting people. But he was still in a great bewilderment as to what was to come next. He realized now, as he had been too angry to do before, that the cause for anger was not *all* on one side. He remembered some of his words to Miss Parkhurst and acknowledged to himself that they were not the words that ought to be spoken by a gentleman to a lady, under any circumstances.

He was somewhat at a loss what to do next. To be sure, he had told her that she was the one who would have to apologize. But he began to feel that the apologies must at least be mutual. He grew almost as angry as before while he thought of this necessity. He was a gentleman who liked to be comfortable and good-natured, and generally was so. But then he, by no means, liked to have his will crossed. Had not one of Cora Parkhurst's charms been that she yielded so gracefully and sweetly to his stronger nature? Just a trifle too ready had her yielding been, where other people were concerned, but he had generally managed that to his satisfaction, until the coming in of this new acquaintance.

"The puppy!" he said, in a great heat and rage, as he thought of the one to whom he chose to attribute all his discomfort. "I will not have that, at any rate," he said, compressing his lips. "I shall tell her that. My words might have been better chosen, of course, but at the same time I totally and utterly object, and shall continue to do so, to this new freak of hers. I shall not endure it again, and a miserable amount of silly nonsense will I have to hear because of it."

And again he thought of that friend of

his, Wells Horton, and the raillery he would have to endure from him. He decided to make a hurried call on Miss Parkhurst before banking hours, for in his heart he felt a trifle worried, lest she might not be in a forgiving mood. She had shown an unaccountable degree of obstinacy of late, and he was not inclined to endure a whole day of suspense, for you are to remember that, with all his faults and failings (and they were not few nor small), he had this title to respect — he had chosen the lady in question from all others because he loved her. I do not say that he did not love himself a trifle better than he did her. You know very well that there are natures who do not and cannot reach above themselves. This is especially apt to be the case with those who have never given themselves up, body and soul, to the worship of the one Supreme Lover who forgot *himself* so utterly as to leave heaven for us. Mr. Tracy knew nothing of this kind of loving, nor indeed of that higher type of human love that is akin to this. He simply thought more of Miss Parkhurst than he did of anyone, *except* himself. But so long as he thought this was love, he is to be respected.

He had his plan of operation arranged to his satisfaction when the boardinghouse servant tapped at his door and produced a note that had been left by Timmy Hughes a moment before. Mr. Tracy took it eagerly. Timmy Hughes was Miss Parkhurst's favorite errand boy. Then he read the note which that lady had written as she thought this trouble all over the night before. He was a good deal touched with it; he had not expected so gentle and kindly a forgiveness. At the same time, it was not good for him. He was too selfish in his nature to be benefited by such words. On the contrary, he began to feel, more than ever, that he had been right and the lady wrong, and that the extraordinary nature of the case had demanded the sharp words he spoke — he called them "sharp" now, not rude. He read it over the second time, with long pauses between the sentences. By this time he had decided that he would not call before banking hours; he would simply write her a note. He would write it at once, and drop it in the nearest lamp post as he passed downtown. That would be less embarrassing than a call.

He spent very little time over his note and was much less excited over it than was Miss Parkhurst when she got it into her own hands. Her discomfort had increased with the morning, for as she thought it all over again, she realized that Mr. Tracy must have been very angry indeed to say to her just what he did, and that before she left him she took the precise course calculated to make an angry man more angry. Perhaps he was even so offended that he would refuse to read her gentle little note, and she should receive it back unopened! She shivered over this possibility — her heart was in this matter, and she had by nature a larger heart than Mr. Tracy. So it was with an eager, nervous grasp that she took this letter from her young sister's hand. Her manner called forth this word of reproof from the sister:

"Don't devour it, Cora, before you get it opened. It is only from George, and I am sure you have had a hundred such. I venture to say that it is nothing more formidable than a ride or a hop, or something of that sort. I wish you two would get married. I should think you would get tired of each other, waiting so long."

After this logical idea she went away and left her sister to the privacy that she needed. This was the note:

DEAR CORA:

My pen almost hesitates over that word, for you certainly tried me to an alarming extent last night. However, I am glad to see that the repentant mood came upon you early. Yes, I forgive you, of course. But equally, of course, you will not put me to so hard a test again. I don't mean about leaving me alone on the street; that was certainly bad enough, but not so trying by far as the other part. I will say here all I wish to on that disagreeable subject, and we need not allude to it again: I shall never want to hear of my promised wife so far forgetting what is due to herself and her position as to make a public talk, no matter how brief nor upon what subject. On this thing we must be agreed. I am willing to believe that you were carried away by an enthusiasm that you imagine to be born of religion. I do not understand these fancies, but of course you were sincere in them. The only point of importance is that they must not carry you captive again. I shall be in this evening, and, by the way, there is a very good opera. I will come on time to take you to it. As ever,

GEORGE

There were no tears in Miss Parkhurst's

eyes as she finished reading this remarkable note. Her face looked utterly unlike tears. Neither did she look offended. The hurt was too deep for that look. But there was that in her face that told she was beginning to understand what she might, and ought to, have known two years ago, that she was the promised wife of a man who had a deep, settled, and persistent antagonism to every development of Christian life, and that he meant to fight all such developments with an unfaltering will. She closed the note thoughtfully and went about her work with a strangely bewildered feeling as to how to take the next step. But her tired heart was thankful for this one thing, that there was no question within her but that the next step *must* be taken.

20

MYSTERIES AT WORK

There is a good deal of time consumed in this world in planning for events that never occur. Sometimes I cannot help feeling that it would be an immense convenience, to say the least, if we could only know the end from the beginning. A knowledge of what was to come would have saved Miss Parkhurst from a weary day of arranging and rearranging for that interview with Mr. Tracy. No, on second thought, it would but have added to her trouble and anxiety and given her sleepless nights and tearful hours. On the whole, things were doubtless better as they are than as I would have made them.

Mr. Tracy did not call on the evening in question in time for the opera. In fact, he did not call at all. Into the dignity and aristocratic rush of business that obtains in a flourishing bank came one of those little papers that slips so quietly through this world of ours with an electric voice, and it said in six words that which revealed a lifetime of pain:

"Mother very low! Come at once!"

Now it so happened that there was one person on earth whom Mr. Tracy loved almost better than he did himself, and that one person was his mother. He looked at his watch and then at the traveler's guide in the morning paper, then he went with it to the inner office to consult with his superior. All the time there was such a stricken look on his face that you would have pitied him, however vexed you may be with him. There was need of haste, for the paper told of a three o'clock express, and it was already two.

So it came to pass that at eight o'clock, instead of sitting by Miss Parkhurst's side in the opera house as he had planned, he was curled in a dismal heap in the corner seat of a railroad car, whirling toward Boston, and only wishing that he could fly, so slowly did they seem to move. He had been mindful of Miss Parkhurst; he had written underneath the telegram these words:

"This just arrived. I must get the three o'clock train."

Then twisting it, had hailed the first boy who passed and sent it to her. But the boy loitered, as some boys will, and the consequence was the three o'clock train had been gone for an hour when she received the word.

You are not to suppose Miss Parkhurst a hardhearted girl when I tell you that she gave a little sigh of relief as she read this note. It was not that she did not sympathize with him; it was not that she would not have saved him from this trouble, if she could have done so; but, since she could not, it was surely no harm to remember that it gave her more time to strengthen her heart and determine just what right was, and to do nothing rashly.

The week which followed was a peculiarly hard one for Mr. Tracy. The scenes through which he had to pass ran directly athwart his unspoken rule of life, to have a free and easy life, without thought for the morrow and its vexations. The vexations were upon him — nay, the downright anxiety and trouble, and they would not be shaken off by a walk in the fresh air and a few puffs of cigar smoke.

His mother was dying. He said "Nonsense!" to his sister, when she asserted, with a burst of tears, that there was no hope; spoke roughly to his father; told his mother that she must not think of giving up; that they were all frightened at their shadows; called the doctor a confounded ninny, and advised the sending for three others, all of different medical schools. Yet in his very heart he believed that they were right, and there was no hope for his mother.

A good, tender mother she had been all his life, with a capacity for devising and carrying out loving, sacrificing plans for her children that was nothing short of the marvelous. A Christian mother she had been in the truest sense of that word, and her son, as he saw her follow him with wistful gaze, knew perfectly that her heaviest pain in this her hour of trial was the thought of him. He knew that she felt the young and timid sister and the boy brother to be infinitely safer and more easily left than he. He knew he had it in his power to make her very happy for the last time in life, by whispering in her dulling ear that he had taken her Savior for his friend and helper, and yet he did not do it.

Verily, human love is a weak and mysterious thing. And yet, possibly, I wrong him; I do not think he realized that he had it in his power to make her closing hours blessed. He looked upon conversion as a strange and mysterious something that must come to him from without, and with which his will had nothing to do. So at times he was half vexed with her for desiring him to have an experience outside of himself.

"They are all an inconsistent set," he muttered as he paced the dining room alone, having just come from the wistful, clasping hand of his mother. "They talk about conversion as an experience that comes only from God, and then blame people for not having it. Why on earth doesn't the Lord convert me, if he wants me to be converted?"

Of course I do not mean to hint that Mr. Tracy believed this nonsense, for he really was gifted with common sense, and he knew perfectly well that God had not chosen to make a machine of him, subject to strings and wheels and bands, without an original motion of his own. No mortal would have resented such a change of plans more quickly than Mr. Tracy, and yet he took refuge behind this poor subterfuge, or pretended to. Still, I admit there was mystery about it, to his mind, and there always would be so long as he spent his time in trying to understand that with which he had nothing to do and passing over in contemptuous indifference the part that was plain to him. The simple truth was, he had not the slightest desire to be a Christian;

all his tastes and inclinations ran in another channel. He was decidedly of the earth, earthy. But he would have liked to please his mother, and it irritated him that he was unable to do so. It seemed necessary to lay the blame somewhere, and, as he was not accustomed to blaming himself, there was no resource but to blame his Creator.

So he went on, sitting much with his mother, taking his share of the watching during the long dreary nights, feeling, in spite of himself, the solemnity of the shadow of death creeping over him, yet trying with all the force of his nature to shake it off, and keeping himself in a state bordering on anger with everybody and everything.

Very little chance had that mother to say anything now. It must have been a happy thought to her that she had not left her work until this hour of weakness, but that of late every loving motherly letter that went from her room to her distant son had pulsed with the eager longing of her heart to see her son safe in the fold. Now her voice was almost gone, and the most that she could give was a low whispered hope that she should have her firstborn with her again in heaven. These wistful appeals he invariably answered by soft kisses pressed on the hot cheeks and lips — tender, clinging kisses, but only *kisses,* not promises. Yet the memory of the disappointed look in her eyes sometimes drove him half wild when he went to the silence of his own room to get rest and sleep.

The end came suddenly. How strange it is, that, however much one may be watching for and dreading the coming of the angel of death, still his coming is a bitter surprise, he had not thought it would be this morning, or tonight. He sat alone beside his mother. She was sleeping, and more quietly than it was her wont to do. A distant clock had just rung out twelve solemn strokes, and, Mr. Tracy, who had risen to shade the lamp more carefully, as he tiptoed back to his seat beside her, looked at his mother's face and stopped, and it seemed to him that his heart stopped beating. He had never looked upon the face of one dying. Yet, as by swift instinct, he knew that death was there.

"Mother," he said, and even then he noticed the strange sound there was in his own voice. "Mother, don't look so! What is it? Can't I get you something, or somebody? What is it?"

"It is heaven!" she said, and her voice

was clear and ringing, not at all as it had been during the last week. "No, George, I want nothing, only this: See to it that you come home in time."

And then, he roused out of the spell which seemed to hold him, rang the nurse's bell, sent for his father, rang the servant's bell, ordered the doctor to be summoned with all speed, brought ammonia and camphor and the most pungent restoratives, and worked with a fierceness and a determination that made the frightened lookers-on shudder. His mother spoke no more, breathed no more, but lay there still and smiling, just as she had looked when she said "It is heaven," and yet with the solemnity that she had looked when she said that other sentence that would ring for so many long nights and weary days through his brain, "See to it that you come home in time."

So the end was reached. Mr. Tracy's mood changed after there was no more chance to see his mother's smile, changed to that of sullen vindictiveness. He felt wronged, almost insulted. Why should *his* mother have died? Other mothers lived to old age. He had planned that his mother was to visit him when he had a home of his own. In short, this rude stranger had

266

broken in on a whole array of plans and ruthlessly held sway until he made it impossible ever in that direction to plan again. A most unhappy son and brother did Mr. Tracy prove the few remaining days that he spent at the homestead, so hopelessly solemn, not to say sullen, that the grief-stricken father, who was trying hard to keep from sinking, was fain to avoid him, and I am obliged to confess that it was with an actual sigh of relief that father and sister turned away from the departing train that bore him homeward.

Meantime, he had not forgotten Miss Parkhurst. Almost every evening a line had been sent to her, full of gloomy forebodings and dismal repinings over the threatened shadow. She, on her part, was very tender and sympathetic, and the cloud that had risen between them seemed to have lost itself in this real trouble. Curiously enough, the strongest feeling that Miss Parkhurst had, when she thought of Mr. Hammond and her conversation with him, was a sense of thankfulness that he had kept her from revealing more than she had of their estrangement. She had felt so touched by his sympathy, she was so freehearted naturally, that she had been on the very verge of telling him the whole story. It was so pleasant now to think that he had kindly checked her, and that no one but George and herself knew aught about it. She told Mr. Hammond the story of her friend's impending trouble and heard his earnestly expressed sympathy, and then they two had engaged to pray that the cloud might have a very silvery lining; that, indeed, it might be the means of leading him to a better sense of life and a higher reaching after comfort and happiness.

It chanced that the letter containing the news of his actual bereavement did not reach her so early as it should, and he was but a few hours' ride away when she sat with the sympathetic tears dropping on her cheek, reading the bitter story. Mr. Hammond was again the first one to extend his sympathy. He called with a business message for the mother and met her as she came downstairs.

"Oh, Mr. Hammond," she said, coming forward as one who had learned to expect sympathy from him, "Mrs. Tracy is dead, and George is nearly heartbroken. He loved his mother as I think few young men do."

"It is a heavy loss," said this young man, with tender, tremulous voice, and eyes that were humid. It was nine years since he had buried *his* mother, and the name was so dear to him that he could not speak it now without a trembling of lips.

It was the evening for prayer meeting, and they walked down to the church together, talking all the way about this matter. Miss Parkhurst, someway, had a feeling that Mr. Hammond was an elder brother, who was immensely interested in George and herself.

"The Lord has many ways of calling his own," he said, as they neared the church. "This may be his chosen method of enticing your friend within his fold." This was his answer to her expressed fear that the trial would have a tendency to harden the young man more against religion.

It was not ten minutes after they left the house that Mr. Tracy rang the bell violently and received with frowning face the intelligence that Cora had gone to prayer meeting.

"I had forgotten that miserable meeting," he said discontentedly. "I should have thought Cora would have waited for me. I told her I was coming."

"Then your letter couldn't have reached her," the mother said, ready as a mother always is to find excuse for her daughter. "In fact, I am sure it didn't, for she told me not an hour ago about getting the news of your mother's —"

"I know," he said, interrupting her hastily.

Mr. Tracy was one of those strange human beings who, a trouble once having actually fallen upon them, want as little as possible said about it. Then he betook himself in all haste and speed to the Harvard Street prayer meeting. Cora he must see as soon as possible, and he was in no mood to loiter the time away until the close of meeting. He took a seat near the door and waited with what patience he could for that to pass in which he conceived that he had an earthly interest. It was just two weeks since he sat there before. A great deal can transpire in two weeks, and the later events that had come to him had been of such a nature as to make the earlier ones retire into the background. He hardly remembered that his last meeting with Cora had ended in a quarrel. He simply knew that his heart was sick and sore, and that he needed soothing and petting. She knew just how to give him this to his satisfaction.

This was not such a meeting as you have formerly attended in Harvard Street Church. During these two weeks the Spirit of God had come very near to the Harvard people; I doubt if they will ever again have just such meetings as they used to have.

Something happened that recalled Mr. Tracy sharply to the present. It was the sound of the voice that he was pleased to think belonged solely to him.

"I have found Christ very precious to me this week." This simple sentence was all she said, and yet what a whirl it raised in the brain of one listener! In an instant that annoying past rose before him, and it had lost none of its importance by reason of being for a time forgotten. It was simply forgotten because he looked upon it as a thing of the past that was not to occur again. He had supposed that his wish was law in this matter, and however annoyed, or even actually angry, Miss Parkhurst might be about it, the idea that she would composedly do again the thing that he had expressly declared must not be done had not for a moment presented itself to him.

I shall not attempt to describe the fever of indignation into which he worked himself. The manner in which he had chosen to accept the teachings of the last two weeks had not tended to help him in this experience. He heard not a single other word that was spoken during the half hour that followed. He gave himself up to the arrangements of the next scene. He should wait for her as usual and meet her as quietly as though she had not angered him beyond endurance. They would have no more outside exhibitions, but, in the course of their walk home, he would say to her with the utmost quietness and plainness that this thing had gone on quite as far as was at all necessary; that she must decide then and there whether she really did intend to move in exact opposition to his expressed wish, not to say command. If she did, it would be better for their lives to part there, before further trouble grew out of it.

Thus coolly he planned, seeming to have an idea that the day when wives were simply dutiful subjects of a stronger will had returned again. Let me tell you a strange thing about this young man. Can you understand that this excitement of feeling had its outgrowth in jealousy? He was actually jealous of her Christian life; of this "presence" that he did not understand, and that she said in a tone of such quiet assurance that she felt. He wanted her to feel no presence that he did not understand and sympathize with. He wanted her to be content with him. So long as religion had only been to her a name and a certain sense of propriety and respectability, he was content to let it alone. But the moment it became a loving, pervading idea, he hated it. Yet this was the man who had heard only so recently that solemn sentence, "Be sure that you come home in time!" Verily, he was traveling very far away from home now. And at that very moment, two hearts were praying that the journey home might be already begun.

The benediction spoken, Mr. Tracy rushed out and stepped a little in the shadow. He knew he was not expected there, and he was in no mood to meet anyone. Ten minutes before, little Timmy Hughes had sauntered that way, and into the very shadow that Mr. Tracy essayed to step, he had thrown the peel from his last quarter of orange. A strange thing it was in this chapter of tragedy, if anyone could have traced it, that the giver of the orange was Miss Cora Parkhurst. On that very bit of orange, no larger than a penny, Mr. Tracy stepped. In an instant his foot slipped, and his forehead struck against the sharp projecting corner of the stone window seat.

That excited brain, with its dark, angry whirl of thoughts, how utterly unprepared it was to endure a blow. The one who caught him as he fell, and who supported him while a carriage could be called, and who went to his boardinghouse with him and spent the night — that anxious, troubled night at his unconscious bedside — was Mr. Hammond.

21

WORK DONE BY THE MASTER

Now all the plans and fears and hopes were changed. What a wonderful and terrible thing a little bit of orange peel can become! Oh, the days and nights that followed! The old story of pain and fear and agony, of apprehension to be lived over. So many people know all about it.

Miss Parkhurst was taking her first lessons. Her life had been one long stretch of sunlight. She felt that the night had dropped down on her suddenly without any twilight warning.

Mr. Tracy's sickness was very sad in some respects. He was very friendless for a young man who had such a host of friends. There was no mother to come to him, and he had never been sick before without feeling the touch of her tender hand all about him. The young sister could not come, for the father had sickened almost immediately after his son's departure and needed all the strength and wisdom she had. But he missed none of them except in a wild, delirious way.

There was little doubt that his thoughts were busy with the past in some of its forms. Those about him did not understand what his fancies were and puzzled in vain over the probable meaning of the constantly and earnestly repeated sentence: "See to it that you come home in time." "Mother said so; I *must* do it," he said to Mr. Hammond on one of these occasions, fixing anxious, troubled eyes on his face, and thereupon Mr. Hammond concluded that he understood it, and that the sick brain was busy with the scenes of childhood and anxious over some command of his mother's — perhaps a command that was disobeyed and had come back from childhood memories to haunt him. He tried, on the strength of this interpretation, to soothe the troubled sufferer, assuring him that he should certainly go. They would help him to start in ample time to get home. If he had known what home was meant and felt the solemnity of his promised help, it would have made him tremble. There would have seemed to him need of haste, for there was scarcely a hope that the thread of life would not snap.

The manner in which Mr. Hammond devoted himself to the sick man, who had not by any means been his friend, was a matter of wonderment to many a looker-on. Every moment that could be spared from business was devoted to him, and far into the night, nearly every night, he was the alert, careful watcher. Even Miss Parkhurst, in the midst of her tearful thanksgivings over this marked care, was filled with surprise as to its cause — its causes, I should have said. They were fourfold.

First, the sick man's helpless and friendless condition appealed to his heart; so many friends to spend evenings with him at the opera, at parties and sleigh rides, and entertainments of all sorts; so few who had the ability or the inclination to give him intelligent, self-sacrificing care. Then, too, he had just buried his mother. Once Mr. Hammond was sick with a fever, and it was a year after his mother's grave had closed over, but he remembered, even after the lapse of so many years, the sick longing that he felt to have one touch of that mother's hand. Even that experience was being visited in blessing on Mr. Tracy's head. Then, too, he had a great pity in his heart for Miss Parkhurst. The sunny life had been so full of trials lately, and she seemed so like a grieved and astonished child; he had an unselfish desire to help and comfort her.

Finally, there was a sad, sore feeling at his heart that this life was slipping away, and there was a whole long array of neglected opportunities staring him in the face; times when, if he had but endured what was distasteful and cultivated a kindly interest in this young man, instead of holding him aloof, he might have helped him. Who could be sure that he might not have saved him? So he waited with patient, prayerful watching, in the hope and longing that the quiet interval would come when reason would resume her way long enough for him to say, "Forgive me, and let me speak a word for my Master."

Meantime, almost of necessity, he became the communicating link between the sickroom and the anxious watcher at her home. She had neither the physical endurance nor the wisdom sufficient to make her a helpful nurse, and her anxious mother eagerly decided that it was best for her to keep entirely aloof; glad in her heart that the peculiar nature of the young man's sickness made him oblivious to all sights and sounds. For who could tell what might not develop from a sickroom? Mrs. Parkhurst's horror of infection was such that she imagined even a brain fever might suddenly change into smallpox or some other horrid disease, so she willingly and thankfully stayed away. And Mr. Hammond, knowing how much he was depended upon, how utterly his word was trusted, and feeling an unutterable pity for the sad-hearted girl, accepted the situation and acted the part of friend and brother to the utmost.

"It is very strange indeed," she said, with a heavy sigh, as after having come with a message from Mr. Tracy's room, he waited while Mrs. Parkhurst made up a basket of sickroom comforts. This woman had her place in life. If she dreaded and shunned sickness, there was still a basket ready to fill, and a shelf on her storeroom where it belonged, and she seemed to know by a sort of instinct what ought to go into it for the sick and suffering. Since her basket did what her presence could never have done, gave help and comfort, may she not be forgiven for withholding the latter?

"It is very strange indeed! I cannot understand it! I have puzzled over it until my head whirls. Here I have wasted my life, made it full of little foolish nothings, and all this time there was nothing to hinder me from work. Now that I am eager and anxious to do all that I can, and at this time when there is so much to do, and my girls so need the help that I can give them, I am so troubled and sad that I seem unable to think of anything. It seems so strange that I should be led in this way at just this time."

Now I think that Miss Parkhurst fully expected an encouraging answer from the gentleman. She was depressed and troubled. She could not rise to the heights of restful faith. She had been too long a stranger to trustfulness to rest easily, but she knew the way of such natures as Mr. Hammond's. She could fancy the assuring words that he would speak, the calm, cheerful reminder that the Lord could take care of his own work. She could not use such language herself, because she had not learned to feel it, but knowing that the man before her had long lived a very different life from hers, and knowing that he meant such words in his very soul, it helped and tested her to hear them.

But Mr. Hammond had been working very hard and sitting up at nights, taking heavy responsibilities. He sympathized with Miss Parkhurst's depressed feelings more than he liked to admit, even to himself. The ways of Providence seemed very strange to him. He had been praying and working for his boys for many weary months. Now he was just beginning to hope for them. The strongest and most hopeless one had deserted the enemy's ranks, and the hearts of the others seemed more impressionable. It had seemed just the time for extra effort and attention. He had planned so much that he intended to do for them. He had been so full of work and courage. To give up all these plans and sit quietly down most of the time with folded hands in a sickroom required a stretch of faith beyond which his blind eyes could not take him, and he answered with a sigh.

The bell tolled for evening meeting.

"Shall you try to go?" he asked Miss Parkhurst, and she answered quickly:

"I can't. I tried that last week, and I am so weak and nervous, so anxious, that it is impossible for me to sit still. I have lost all control of myself, I think, and I know my girls are watching me, and that makes the matter worse. No, I shall not try to go. It seems very sad that I cannot work, now that my heart is in it."

Despite his effort to feel differently, it seemed so to Mr. Hammond. He meant to interest Larry Bates in this meeting, at least he had hoped to get him to be present, and he knew that Lester was at work for Will Gordon and looked to him for help. How strange it was that he should have, instead, to spend the evening with a man who had not even been a friend, held there by a cord that was very strong to a nature like his. He was conscious there was a responsibility to assume, and that he knew both what to do and how to do it, which was more than could be said of the few who were at hand to help. His sigh was more long-drawn than before as he said:

"It is certainly a very strange Providence." And then he rallied just enough to say, "But we must try to trust," saying it with a very wan smile, as if he meant, however dark the day, and however discouraging the prospect, they would hope that it would come right somehow, even though it did require a heavy strain on one's faith. And it is just such meager, lowborn feelings as these that the Master is obliged to accept from us as faith.

"Well, good night," Mr. Hammond said at last, as the basket was pronounced ready. "Try to keep up as good courage as you can. You shall hear at once if there is any difference between this and morning. No, I do not expect to have him. I have engaged to watch tonight." Then he hurried away, leaving Miss Parkhurst thankful indeed for his help and his faithfulness. But oh, *so* heavyhearted!

There were two letters written that evening, and you shall have a copy of each of them. The first was Miss Parkhurst's, addressed to Mr. Hammond. It was written an hour after prayer meeting. It ran thus:

MR. HAMMOND:

My dear friend, I feel very much ashamed. I must have appeared a very weak and worthless Christian in your eyes this evening. I do not say in the eyes of my Savior, for he who knows just how weak and foolish I am knows also that I love him, though I may not appear to do so. But to think that I should have the folly to suppose that he could not take care of my girls without me, when he has had to do it without my help all these years!

I have just heard from the meeting, I wonder if you have? Your Lester St. John took a decided stand. And, don't you think, May and Fanny Horton both said they wanted to be Christians! Sarah came to see me afterward, and she says Fanny thought there must be something in the religion that could sustain me at this time. That makes me very humble, for I feel that I have not let it sustain me as it would have done. But isn't it blessed in all this trouble to think that the girls are coming — my girls whom I have *mis*led so long? Celia, too, the last one for whom I had hope, sends me word that she is thinking.

And oh, one thing was so kind and precious that I must tell you of it. Fanny and May sent me word that they were learning to pray, and that they would pray for me, and for my dear friend tonight. God bless them for that! I feel stronger. I think God will save George's life.

Do you know that next to him I shall know that I am to thank you? I wish I could tell you how very grateful I feel to you. It does not seem as strange to me as it did — this Providence, I mean, I have a faint glimmering feeling of great things that may be brought to pass out of it. I suppose there is a place higher than that, which is to *know* God will bring to pass great things for those who trust him out of all pain. But he is very patient with my blunderings.

The letter closed abruptly, for the reason

that there came a messenger from Mr. Hammond bringing a note to her, and she waited only to see that there was no worse news than she had had during the day. Then she sent her letter back by the same messenger, and sat down to read what Mr. Hammond had to tell her. This was his note:

DEAR FRIEND:

You came to a broken reed for comfort this evening. I can only hope that you were driven to the strong Arm and are resting there. What a foolish thing this is, what we dignify by the name of *faith*. It seems we can only trust just as far as we can see the shadow of the footsteps.

I have had a wonderful evening. It began in gloom; the silent companion on the bed was more quiet and restful than usual; in my ignorance I feared it to be a bad sign (let me tell you right here that it is the most hopeful one we have had for many a day), and my heart was very heavy. I was motioned to the door to meet Will Gordon. His father had sent him to inquire and to offer help. That being done, he tarried for a moment, then, turning, took my hand and said:

"Mr. Hammond, I wanted you to know that the question is settled. I have gone over to the King's side." Just that, and he rushed away. Can you imagine what that was to me? My boy Will, for whom I have so longed and prayed, coming to me at the moment when my heart was filled with questioning thoughts as to why I should not be permitted to get him to go to the meeting with me this evening as I had planned.

Will was scarcely gone when the boy brought a drop letter from Larry. It was characteristic — only two lines: "It is done at last, and when I decide anything, you know it is decided." I knew what he meant. Two boys! Think of it! And I in my weakness had spent this day in lamentation. Oh, Miss Parkhurst, you and I are not the right sort of teachers yet. We must remember that we are only *under*teachers, assistants, and because we are trammeled, it is no sign that the Principal cannot do his work well.

Now, my friend, you will think we had victory enough for one evening. But in the course of the next half hour came Wells Horton to see Mr. Tracy. He shivered a little as he stood looking at him. Then, to my surprise, he quoted, solemnly, " 'There is but a step betwixt me and death.' You did not know that I was familiar with a Bible verse, did you?" he asked, noticing my surprised look. "But I tell you I have thought of but little else since this accident. I have passed through a strange conflict since that time, but I wish the dear fellow knew that I have learned to pray, and that I am praying God to give him back to us."

Dear Miss Parkhurst, I tell you this in detail because I think it will answer some of your sad questions tonight. God is calling these young men to himself, and, strangely enough, the means that he is using, in this instance at least, is this accident that has seemed to us so utterly dreadful. What may he not be going to bring to pass through it? My faith has taken a higher reach. It would be strange if it could not, with all these helps to lift one. I believe that God will give your friend to us in a renewed life, not physically only, but spiritually. Take heart of grace. There are new voices praying tonight that have never prayed before, and they are asking for him. The Lord forgive us for trembling and doubting and feeling that our ways of working were the only ways. There are depths of mercy that we cannot understand, but let us learn to trust.

There was a little note that followed this, a hurriedly written sentence on the back of an envelope. These words:

Midnight. The doctor is here. He says there has been a change. The breathing is becoming natural, the pulse is better, and he is almost certain that all will be well. The Lord reigns and is all-powerful and wonderful in His loving-kindness.

It was after reading that sentence that Miss Parkhurst fell on her knees, and the prayer that she prayed for Mr. Tracy was such as God hears.